Jake met Carolina's steely gaze. "I've been way out of line. I jumped to conclusions and made a fool of myself."

She gazed at him, the anger subsiding as a look of pleading burned in her eyes. "I don't care what you think of me, Jake, but I'm begging you to contact your father, soon, before it's too late. It would mean the world to him—and to me."

Jake's insides twisted. It was tearing him apart to look into her eyes and refuse her, but she had no idea what she was asking of him.

"I'll think about it." That was the most he could promise.

"Then I guess I'll have to settle for that for now." She turned away and resumed packing.

A protective urge hit him hard and fast. "I know I don't really have a say in the matter, but I'd really like it if you'd spend the rest of the week at the Silver Spur."

"Why?"

To keep her safe. To keep her close. He wasn't sure exactly which need was stronger at this moment.

AMBUSH AT DRY GULCH

JOANNA WAYNE

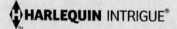

To my very patient and supportive editor, Denise Zaza, who believed in me enough to stand by me during recent health problems, and to my wonderful readers, who came to love the Lamberts and the Daltons (especially Texas rounder R.J. Dalton) as much as I do.

Recycling programs for this product may not exist in your area.

ISBN-13: 978-0-373-74968-3

Ambush at Dry Gulch

Copyright © 2016 by Jo Ann Vest

Printed in U.S.A.

www.Harlequin.com

Joanna Wayne began her professional writing career in 1994. Now, more than fifty published books later, Joanna has gained a worldwide following with her cutting-edge romantic suspense and Texas family series, such as Sons of Troy Ledger and Big "D" Dads. Joanna currently resides in a small community north of Houston, Texas, with her husband. You may write Joanna at PO Box 852, Montgomery, TX 77356, or connect with her at joannawayne.com.

Books by Joanna Wayne

Harlequin Intrigue

Big "D" Dads: The Daltons

Trumped Up Charges
Unrepentant Cowboy
Hard Ride to Dry Gulch
Midnight Rider
Showdown at Shadow Junction
Ambush at Dry Gulch

Sons of Troy Ledger

Cowboy Swagger
Genuine Cowboy
AK-Cowboy
Cowboy Fever
Cowboy Conspiracy

Big "D" Dads

Son of a Gun
Live Ammo
Big Shot

Visit the Author Profile page at Harlequin.com for more titles.

CAST OF CHARACTERS

Carolina Lambert—The stunning widow of wealthy rancher and oil man Hugh Lambert, and R.J. Dalton's favorite neighbor. She thinks her life is complete until she meets Jake Dalton.

Jake Dalton—Rancher, single parent and R.J. Dalton's oldest son, the only son who has not reconnected with him.

R.J. Dalton—He's lived his life on his terms, but after being diagnosed with a brain tumor, he only wants to reconnect with his children and grandchildren.

Lizzie Dalton—Jake's teenage daughter.

Mildred Caffey—Good friend of Carolina Lambert who is being harassed by her ex-husband.

Thad Caffey—Blames Carolina for his wife divorcing him.

Mary—Jake's mother and R.J. Dalton's first wife.

Edna—Jake's housekeeper, though she's more like family than an employee.

Aidan Bastrop—State representative, friend of Jake Dalton and a supporter of Carolina's charitable work, including the Saddle-Up Program.

Tague, Damien and Durk Lambert—Carolina's adult sons.

Sheriff Garcia—He's determined to stop Thad Caffey before he harms Carolina or Mildred.

Sara Billings—A Saddle-Up volunteer.

Peg Starling—A Saddle-Up volunteer.

Chapter One

Carolina Lambert shifted in the porch swing so that she could look her neighbor R.J. Dalton in the eye while they talked. He rocked back and forth in his chair, sometimes looking at her, more often staring into space.

Her heart ached at the way his body grew weaker each day. He had already beaten the odds by more than two years, but the inoperable tumor in his brain was relentless. It was only a matter of time and yet there was a peace to his spirits that she envied.

He sipped his black coffee, his wrinkled hands so unsteady that it took both of them to hold his mug. "I reckon Brit told you that you better get over here and check on the old man while she took Kimmie in for her checkup."

"No one has to coax me. Spending time with you is always my pleasure," Carolina said truthfully.

But he was right. Even with a precious baby girl to keep her busy, his daughter-in-law Brit had pretty much taken over the job of coordinating the family's schedule so that R.J. was never alone for more than a few minutes at a time.

"I swear you dropped off Saint Peter's coattail, Carolina. You're the best danged neighbor a scoundrel like me ever had. Best looking, too. Can't believe you're still running around single. Hugh's been dead what? Three? Four years now?"

"Four and a half."

"That's a long time to put your life on hold."

"My life's not on hold. I'm busy all the time with my family, friends like you and countless projects."

"Not the same as having a lover."

"Now, what are you doing even thinking about lovers at your age?"

"I'm not dead yet. If I was thirty years younger and not playing hide-and-seek with the grim reaper, I'd be after you quicker than hell can scorch a feather."

"You've done more than your share of chasing women, Reuben Jackson Dalton."

"I caught a few mighty fine ones, too."

"So I've heard."

He smiled, the wrinkles around his eyes cutting deep into the almost-translucent flesh.

"Lived life on my terms, sorry as it was. By rights I ought to be drowning in regrets. Wasn't for taking your advice about what to do with my ranch, I would be."

"I can't take credit for you turning your life around."

"You don't have to take it, by jiggers. I'm a-givin' it to you. I offered to give you the Dry Gulch Ranch free and clear. You turned me down. Didn't leave me much choice except to try your idea."

"I suggested you leave the Dry Gulch Ranch to your family. That's not a particularly inventive idea."

"Sounded like crazy talk to me. Leave this ranch and what lottery winnings I had left to a bunch of strangers who wouldn't have tipped their hats if I'd passed them on the street."

"Until they got to know you."

He nodded and rubbed his weathered, bony chin. "Blessing was I got to know them. Listen at me, talking about blessings. You have really rubbed off on me. Surprise, ain't it, after me being a worthless rounder most of my eighty-plus ornery years?"

"You were never worthless."

"I done plenty of stuff I'm not proud of, but I must have done something good along the way, like pick the right women to birth and raise my kids. You gotta admit, I got me some real winners. Got the smartest and cutest durned grandkids on the planet, too."

"Next to mine," Carolina teased. "So you really do have no regrets?"

"I'd like to trade a few more years with my family for all the ones I've wasted, but I'm good with what I've got." He turned to watch a woodpecker in a nearby pine tree. "Would be lying if I didn't say I have one other regret, though."

"What is that?"

R.J. scratched his chin, his fingers poking into the loose pads of skin at his neck. "I'd just like the chance to sit around the table and chew the fat with Jake, one-on-one. At least make a stab at getting to know my firstborn, find out why he's so set against being part of the family."

Carolina swallowed hard, feeling his pain and fighting her own swelling anger. R.J. hadn't been much of a father to any of his children when they were growing up, but what kind of adult son could just turn his back on his dying father? She tried not to think ill of anyone, but Jake Dalton was the exception.

She'd gone so far as to call him herself last week, planned to beg if necessary to get him to pay R.J. a visit before it was too late. He'd been cool and aloof, until she'd pushed.

Then he'd struck out at her, accusing her of

having done enough already to screw up R.J. and the rest of the Dalton clan. She might have found out what he meant by that if her temper hadn't flared to the point that she'd hung up on him.

The man was arrogant, coldhearted and infuriating. If his mother was anything like him, no wonder R.J.'s first marriage had ended in divorce.

Of course, so had his other three marriages, so she definitely couldn't absolve R.J. of fault.

"How's your friend Mildred Caffey?" R.J. asked. "Has that no-good, wife-beater ex-husband of hers tried to get in touch with her since he got out of prison?"

"He hadn't the last time we talked, but I know she's worried that he will. It's been good for her that she's been so busy working on a project with me."

"You don't think she'll go back to him, do you?"

"No. She's much smarter and more emotionally stable now then she was when they were together."

"Thanks to you." R.J. swatted at a honeybee that had been flitting among the blossoms of the potted petunias scattered about the porch. "You go around rescuing every stray you see."

"Only the ones who want my help. And

Mildred isn't a stray. She just made some bad choices along the way."

"Sure as shooting, she did. I knew Thad Caffey was bad blood the first time I met him. Don't know why a nice young woman like Mildred ever married a no-account skunk like that."

"Love sometimes blinds people."

"Reckon you're right about…" He stopped midsentence, ran bony, knotty fingers through his thinning hair and stared into space.

He stayed silent so long Carolina feared he was fading into one of the spells he had far too often these days. Times when he drifted into another world, one where he didn't recognize his own family. One where he visited a woman from his past or from his dreams.

Carolina imagined this phantom as a first love, one who had carved out a space in his heart and never fully let go. Perhaps someone he'd loved the way she'd loved Hugh.

Finally R.J. turned and looked at Carolina, his eyes clearer now, as if he'd returned from the secret caches of the memories that had claimed him.

"He's gonna be out to kill you, Carolina."

"Who?"

"Thad Caffey. I was in the courtroom the day the jury found him guilty. I saw the way he looked at you, his face contorted and his eyes wild like he was a panther about to spring. I figured he blamed you for her testifying against him."

"If he thinks I encouraged her, he'd be absolutely right. I won't be intimidated by Thad Caffey."

"Or any other man around these parts." R.J. sputtered a raspy, guttural sound that might have been a chuckle or a cough. "All the same, keep an eye out for trouble."

Carolina looked up at the sound of approaching hooves and gladly let the topic drop as R.J.'s son Adam came riding up on a handsome gray mare. He tipped his hat and dismounted.

"Hope I'm not interrupting anything."

"Absolutely not," Carolina assured him. "Always good to see you."

"And you. Hadley's been talking about having you over for supper one night soon, but she says you're jumping through hoops getting ready for that summer riding-camp program you're organizing."

"I have to be in Austin for their area training session starting tomorrow. This is a busy time."

"Busy myself. Spring on the ranch," Adam said, knowing she'd understand that said it all. He joined them on the porch, stopping to lean against the railing. "Just came by to see if you want to go check out a new foal that was born last night, Dad."

"Long as you don't expect me to ride that mare of yours to the barn."

"Nope. We'll take your truck."

"Good. I'm about as steady as a cat on skates these days. Carolina can go with us. She's always keen on any kind of baby."

"Yes, but I have to beg out today," Carolina said. "Too many errands on my to-do list. But I know you'll be in good hands."

She stood when R.J. did and gave him a quick hug and a kiss on his sallow cheek. Her anger swelled again at the thought of Jake Dalton and his refusal to pay a visit to the Dry Gulch Ranch and R.J. The loss was definitely his.

The Daltons were one terrific family—second in her heart only to her own.

She said her goodbyes and went back to her black Mercedes sports car. Her phone rang before she made it back to the highway.

"Hello."

"Glad I caught you, Carolina. This is Jack Crocker, and I got a bit of bad news for you."

"What's wrong?"

"I'm going to have to back out of hosting that training session here on my ranch next week."

Her spirits plummeted. The arrangements were all made. Ten new summer riding camps opened in two weeks, their first venture into the Austin area. If they canceled the training, they had to cancel the program and disappoint one hundred and fifty young teens from the inner city.

She'd known Jack and his wife for years. They were the first people she'd thought of when she decided to branch out to the Austin area.

"What's happened?" she asked, struggling not to show her disappointment. "Are you sick? Is Betsy?"

"Nope. Me and the wife are fine. Just found out that all the kids and grandkids are coming to town to surprise Betsy for her seventieth birthday. No idea why they didn't tell me before now, 'cept they figured I'd never keep the secret."

"I understand," she said, crushed, but already trying to figure out a plan B.

"Don't you go frettin' about it, though," Jack consoled. "I wouldn't leave you stranded in a ditch without a mule to haul you out. I gave a call to Aidan Bastrop. He took over from there."

"Took over, how?" Aidan was a state representative and a friend, but this time she didn't see how he'd be able to intervene. He didn't own a ranch, and much of the training required that.

"Aidan worked something out with a neighbor of mine. You'll have bigger and better facilities than what you'd have had here."

The knots in her stomach relaxed. She should have known Jack wasn't the type to blow a commitment lightly. The relief lasted for the two seconds it took for him to mutter the name of his replacement.

The last person on earth she would have asked for a favor.

Chapter Two

Jacob Edward Dalton worried the knot in his red-striped tie for about ten seconds before jerking it off and tossing it to a nearby chair. Texas State Capitol building or not, he was going casual. Mid-June and the humidity was already battling the temperature for record highs for this time of year.

He could kick himself for letting Aidan Bastrop talk him into volunteering the Silver Spur for some project he'd never even heard of before now. Nothing like a gaggle of women descending on a ranch to guarantee his wranglers would do more gawking than work.

Not that Jake was against helping out. He gave generously to several causes important to him. But he had a ranch to run and a teenage daughter to corral, neither of which was going particularly well at the moment.

His foreman had been thrown last week when

a rattlesnake spooked his horse. Granger had suffered a broken leg and bruised ribs. The man would be limited in what he could do for the next couple of weeks, though Granger would keep abreast of everything going on around the Silver Spur.

As for his daughter, Lizette, he was considering shipping her off to the Arctic until she cooled down. Her latest state of rebellion had been fueled by his forbidding her to date Calvin Owens.

Calvin was the local bad boy, two years older than Lizzie, and already had a juvenile record for vandalizing the local high school and shoplifting. And that was just what they knew he was guilty of.

Now Lizzie was constantly pushing the house rules and the limits of decency in her wardrobe choices. If her denim cutoffs got any shorter, she might as well skip them altogether. She considered curfews irrelevant and her newly acquired driver's license a proclamation of freedom.

She did a lot better when her grandmother was in the house. But Jake's mother, Mary, was on a European river cruise with a few of the other widows from their church. She was almost eighty, yet some days Jake swore she had more energy than he did. She definitely had more skill in dealing with Lizzie.

Jake headed down the hallway and stopped at the door to Lizzie's bedroom. He tapped softly and lingered a minute, though he didn't expect a response. She hadn't been up before noon once since school let out for the summer.

He took the wide staircase to the first floor and then followed the smell of fresh brew to the kitchen. "Good morning, Edna," he greeted his housekeeper as he poured himself a mug of coffee. "You're here early today."

"Not a lot of use in hanging around my place by myself when I can be up here drinking your coffee and soaking up your air-conditioning."

"Can't blame you for that." And it wasn't as if she had far to come. Jake had built Edna a cabin on his spread after her husband died almost three years ago. The tall big-boned woman had been with him ever since he'd turned his back on a promising medical career and taken over the ranching business right after…

Nope. He was not going there this morning.

Edna handed him a cup of coffee. "You don't look like you're planning to do a lot of ranching today."

"No, but I should be. Instead I'm off to Austin and the capitol building for some meeting that I don't have time for."

"Seems like all those politicians do is meet. What are they yakking about this time?"

"Some project that Aidan Bastrop enlisted my help with."

"I thought you had more on your plate than you can handle with Granger hurt."

"Yep, but this is an emergency of sorts."

Edna opened the refrigerator and started pulling out breakfast items while he finished his coffee. "What is it you've volunteered for? Giving a talk about ranching? Sponsoring an event? Making a donation?"

"I'm donating, all right. Unfortunately it's not just money. It's the ranch."

She looked at him as if he'd lost his mind—which he probably had, at least temporarily. "Donated the ranch? What in blue blazes are you talking about?"

"Actually, it's only the *use* of the ranch, our horses, corrals and some meeting space. And only for five days, starting Wednesday."

"Who borrows a ranch?"

"A group of about thirty women. But don't start having conniptions. You won't have to do a thing."

"Humph. A bunch of strange women taking over the place and no extra work. That'll never happen."

"I'll see that it does," he promised, though

he wasn't fully convinced of that himself. "The house is not included in the loan."

"What are all these women training for, some kind of trail ride?"

"Nope. It's called the Saddle-Up program, or something like that."

"Never heard of it."

"Nor had I, but then it involves teenage girls, so it's outside my realm of expertise. I have enough trouble managing Lizzy."

"Exactly what do they do with these teenagers?"

"According to Aidan's persuasive argument, they give inner-city girls from high-poverty areas one month on a real working ranch over the summer. They teach them to ride, work as a team, take responsibility—that sort of thing."

Edna's hands flew to her ample hips. "Well, why didn't you just say that in the first place? Those kids need a summer on a ranch. When does this training start?"

"Officially—Wednesday."

"This Wednesday? As in two days away?"

"Yes, but like I said. You don't have to do a thing." As if there was a chance Edna wouldn't be in the middle of things.

"You can't ignore guests," Edna said. "It's not the Texas way."

"Maybe not, but I plan to give it my best

shot." Starting today. "A few of the women are coming out to tour the ranch this afternoon, just to get their bearings before the official training begins. If they show up at the house before I get back, give me a call and I'll have one of the wranglers hook up with them."

"You should be here for that," she said. "You never know. Some of those women might be mighty fine-looking."

"I'm sure the wranglers will appreciate that. If you need me, call me."

"You're not leaving without breakfast, are you? I can whip up some bacon and eggs before you finish your coffee."

"No need. I'll grab a bite to eat in town. Best to get on the road now before traffic becomes a pain in the butt. But you can remind my daughter when she finally crawls out of bed that I expect to see her at the dinner table tonight. On time."

Edna stared at him as if he'd spoken in a foreign language. "Lizzie didn't spend the night here last night."

Irritation ground in his gut. "She was here when I went to bed."

"She left you a note on the foyer table that she was spending the night with her friend Angie."

"A note telling me—not asking. Another stunt like this and I'm going to take her keys away."

"Maybe you should just sit down and talk to her first. Take her for a horseback ride and a little teamwork of your own."

"See you at dinner," Jake said. He turned and walked away before he said something he'd be sorry for.

Edna thought talking was the answer to every problem that came along, but she had no idea what he'd been through with Lizzie. If her mother was here...

The old pain swelled inside him, followed by a surge of crusty hardness that allowed him to keep functioning. It was the only way he knew.

When he reached the foyer, he picked up his daughter's note. *Angie broke up with her boyfriend tonight. Needs a friend. I'll spend the night. See ya.*

He'd been home. She should have asked him before she left instead of sneaking away. But then if she'd asked, he'd have said no. At sixteen, she was too young to be driving the dark country roads out to Angie's at night.

If she'd even gone to Angie's.

The sweet, adorable Lizette he'd known once had to live somewhere inside the stranger she'd become. Somehow he had to find a way to reach her.

Instead he was off to a meeting he could do without.

CAROLINA MARCHED UP the steps of the capitol building, fighting the growing agitation that she was forced to accept Jake Dalton's help, mentally debating how she'd handle their initial meeting.

"Slow down," Mildred said. "I'm out of breath trying to keep up with you."

"Sorry. I guess I'm still blowing off steam."

"You are going to be civil to Mr. Dalton, aren't you?"

"I'll try. That's the best I can promise—which is more than he was with me when I called him about paying R.J. a visit."

"You might have caught him at a bad time. Maybe this is his way of making it up to you."

"I seriously doubt that. And if it was just a matter of timing, he's had time to rethink it and contact R.J. Besides, he was the one who made this personal by insinuating I'd done something wrong."

"If he's still upset with you, he certainly wouldn't have volunteered the Silver Spur for the Saddle-Up project."

"I strongly suspect a little quid pro quo was involved. He probably owed a favor to Aidan Bastrop—or wants one from him."

"Whatever his reason, I'm glad the training wasn't canceled," Mildred said. "Now I just hope I can continue to be part of it."

Mildred's voice hinted of angst. Carolina slowed and turned to face her. "Of course you'll be part of it. You've already put in hours and hours of work."

"I know, but…"

"But what?"

"Thad."

Carolina's irritation switched from Jake to Mildred's abusive ex-husband. "Have you heard from him?"

"Last night, near midnight. He sounded as if he'd been drinking."

"What did he want?"

"To see me. He said it's urgent."

"What gall. He almost beat you to death. You're divorced now. You owe him nothing."

"He admitted all that, but he begged me to give him another chance. He says he's a changed man."

"What did you tell him?"

"That it's over and he should go on with his life. But I know Thad. He's not going to accept that. He thinks I belong to him like a piece of property. He always did."

Mildred was clearly disturbed and with good reason. She needed to talk this out, but the meeting was due to start in minutes. "Why didn't you mention this at breakfast or on the drive from the hotel to the capitol?"

"I didn't want to upset you, but then I started to feel guilty about keeping it from you. If you want me to drop out of the training, I'll understand."

"Drop out and let Thad dictate your life. Absolutely not. You can block him from calling you again, and you definitely don't have to see him."

"That doesn't mean he won't cause trouble."

"If he does, we'll contact Sheriff Garcia and he'll have him arrested. The law is on your side. You don't have to put up with Thad's abuse ever again. Now, let's not let Thad Caffey ruin our day. After all, we have Jake Dalton for that," she added with a smile, trying to ease Mildred's tension.

Senator Ralph Baldwin caught up with them just as they reached the door. He pushed it open and held it for them to enter.

"Good morning, Carolina. You look beautiful, as always," he said, practically ogling.

"Thank you. You look nice yourself." She stepped through the door and kept walking. She could definitely do without Ralph's seduction routine this morning.

The senator took her arm and tugged her to a stop. "Why didn't you tell me you'd be here today?"

So she could avoid awkward moments like this one. "I'm just here for a meeting."

"I have a luncheon meeting myself today, but I'm free tonight. Surely you could stay over in Austin and have dinner with me," Ralph said. "I hate to eat alone."

"I'll go on ahead," Mildred said, no doubt mistakenly thinking Carolina would appreciate the privacy.

Carolina turned back to Ralph. "You could always have dinner at home with your wife."

"She's in Midland visiting her parents." He lowered his voice. "Besides, I've told you, we're married in name only and even that will come to an end after the next election."

"Perhaps we'll have dinner then." And perhaps there would be a Dallas snowstorm in August. "I need to go now. Time for my meeting." She hurried away before he had time to reply.

No one seemed to understand that she didn't need a man in her life. She'd been married to Hugh Lambert, bigger than life, a man among men. How could she ever expect to find a man to measure up to him? If she did, it certainly wouldn't be a lowlife philanderer like Ralph Baldwin.

Carolina hurried down the wide halls of the capitol and slipped inside the conference room a few minutes before the scheduled starting time.

Once she was inside, the noise level increased dramatically. A good sign that the volunteers were excited about the project.

Carolina glanced around the room, nodding and smiling at the attendees. This would be her first time to meet many of them, though she'd interviewed every volunteer by phone and had a background check run on them. In every case they were respectable ranchers' wives or experienced riders, active in their communities.

There was much more to providing an enriching summer experience to these teens than just teaching them to ride. She had to make sure the volunteers knew exactly what they were signing up for and that they had a true desire to help and bond with the frequently troubled girls.

She quickly spotted Jake Dalton, standing in a corner by himself. It was only the second time she'd seen him in person, the first being at the Dry Gulch just after R.J. had been diagnosed with an inoperable brain tumor.

The occasion had been less than joyous—the reading of R.J.'s will while he was still alive. Jake had been resentful then, and unlike his half siblings, he apparently still nurtured his grudge.

He had the same ruggedly handsome features as his four younger half-brothers. Tall. Tanned. Broad shouldered. Chiseled jaw. Lean and hard bodied. Blatantly masculine in his ranch-cut sports jacket and shirt that was open at the neck. A bit of gray salted the thick, dark hair around his temples.

About her age, she'd guess, though he might be younger than her fifty-five years. The only obvious negative to his looks was a mouth that looked as if it might have forgotten how to smile. Probably a reflection of having to deal with her this morning.

Only he didn't have to. He could have said no. She knew for a fact he was good at that.

Aidan welcomed the group and talked for only a few minutes before introducing Carolina. Jake Dalton stared at her, looking as shocked as if someone had thrown a glass of ice water in his handsome face.

So he hadn't known he'd be dealing with her and hadn't recognized her before now. That explained a lot. She could start looking forward to five days from hell.

After the introductions, Aidan and Jake excused themselves and left the room, and the rest of the meeting went off without a hitch. The women all seemed capable and excited about the project.

They broke at noon. Carolina, Mildred, Peg Starling and Sara Billings, the four who planned to tour the facilities at the Silver Spur Ranch that afternoon, lingered in the conference room.

"How is it you failed to mention our host was a hunk?" Sara asked.

"And no little gold band on the gorgeous rancher's finger," Peg commented. "Guess that means he's available?"

"I wouldn't know," Carolina said. "Any ideas for lunch that won't eat up too much of our afternoon?"

"There's a French bakery nearby that makes great coffee and sandwiches and the best almond tart I've ever tasted," Sara suggested. "It will be crowded, but service is fast."

"Works for me," Mildred said.

"And for me," Peg added.

"Then the bakery it is," Carolina agreed, ready to get moving before the conversation switched back to Jake's looks or relationship status.

"If you don't mind, I'll get you and Mildred to follow us to our ranch after lunch," Sara said. "It's on the way and we can change into jeans, drop my car off at home and catch a ride with you out to the Silver Spur."

"Can do. Mildred and I brought more appropriate clothes for the ranch, as well. We can change at your place."

"I would have packed much sexier jeans if I'd known Jake Dalton was so good-looking," Peg said.

"You'll be sexy no matter what you wear," Mildred assured the shapely blonde.

Carolina picked up her purse and slung the strap over her shoulder as the door opened and both Aidan and Jake stepped back into the room. She wasn't surprised to see Aidan, but she'd assumed Jake was long gone, possibly trying to figure out an excuse to get out of his commitment to the project.

"I hope everything went well," Aidan said.

"Couldn't have gone better," Carolina assured him.

"Carolina's enthusiasm gets everyone fired up," Sara added.

"I'd love to take you women to lunch," Aidan said, "but I have another meeting at one."

"What about you, Mr. Dalton?" Peg asked flirtatiously.

"I have some errands to take care of in town before I head out," Jake said, keeping his tone businesslike. "I'll give you directions to the ranch. When you get there, my housekeeper, Edna, will hook you up with one of the wranglers. He'll show you around and answer any questions you have."

"That will work out fine," Carolina assured him, keeping her tone as cool and aloof as his had been.

Directions were simple, and she was relieved

when they were finally on their way. Jake was no doubt as eager to be rid of her as she was of him. He was turning them over to a wrangler for today's tour. She suspected that would be his modus operandi for the remainder of the training session.

With luck, she might not even have to see him again.

"I know you think Jake Dalton is a heartless cad," Mildred said as she walked to the car with Carolina.

"Yes, I do."

"You can't blame him too much for not bonding with a father he never really knew. Didn't all of R.J.'s sons feel that way at one point?"

"Yes," she admitted reluctantly, "but that doesn't excuse Jake's behavior. He's the oldest. He should feel some level of responsibility."

"If anyone can change his mind, you will," Mildred said.

"With luck, I won't even have to speak to him."

They were several yards away from her vehicle when Carolina spotted a man leaning against the front fender of her car. He was in ripped jeans and a black muscle shirt, a cigarette dangling from the corner of his mouth. A snake tattoo covered much of his right arm. A pair of aviator sunglasses hid his eyes, but his mouth was twisted into a menacing frown. An uneasy chill crept up her spine.

She glanced around. The parking lot was crowded with cars and pickup trucks, but the closest people she spotted were two men in suits, several rows down, walking in the opposite direction.

When the thuggish-looking man noticed her staring at him, he smiled and nodded as if in greeting.

Mildred grabbed Carolina's wrist and pulled her to a stop. "What are you doing here?" Mildred demanded.

The man flicked his cigarette to the concrete and ground it out with the toe of his right boot. "Waiting on you."

The taunting voice struck a chord and finally Carolina recognized Thad. He'd changed during his four years behind bars. Gained weight. Added a lot of muscle.

Mildred dropped Carolina's wrist and hugged her arms about her own chest, as if protecting herself from Thad's presence. "We no longer have anything to discuss."

"That doesn't sound like much of a welcome for a husband you haven't seen in four years."

"You are no longer her husband," Carolina corrected.

"Stay out of this, Carolina. This is between me and Mildred," Thad snapped.

"Please, Thad. Just go," Mildred pleaded. "I don't want trouble."

"I'm not going anywhere until we talk."

"What part of her not wanting to see you do you not understand? Either you go willingly or I call the cops," Carolina ordered.

"I'm not breaking any laws. This is a public parking lot. So you call anybody you want to."

He left the car and stepped closer, his gaze firmly planted on Mildred, his tone switching from arrogant to loving without missing a beat. "I know I made mistakes, sweetheart, but you can't imagine how much I've missed you. We can start over now. I promise you that things will be different."

Carolina's stomach turned at his meaningless promises. Too little, too late. "Last chance, Thad. If you don't leave this minute, I'm calling 911."

"How about you let Mildred speak for herself? Or are you running her life now the way you run half of Texas?"

Mildred let her arms fall to her side. "I do speak for myself now, Thad. I hope you have changed—for your sake—but we can't go back. I've moved on."

"You know you don't mean that, baby. You

still love me. I still love you. We can work this out."

"We can't. It's over between us, Thad." Her voice trembled, but she didn't back away.

Carolina put a steadying arm around Mildred's waist. "There's your answer, Thad. You can leave now unless you're looking to go back to prison."

"Go to hell, Carolina."

Fury burned in his voice now, his mood turning dark and threatening. He reached out and grabbed Mildred's arm, jerking her toward him. "Don't make me do something I'll be sorry for, Mildred. You know how I get when you make me crazy."

Carolina pulled her cell phone from her handbag. Thad let go of Mildred and grabbed Carolina's wrist with one hand while twisting the phone from her fingers with the other. She heard the clunk as it hit the concrete beneath their feet.

"Is there a problem here?"

Carolina jerked around at the sound of the strong, male voice. She gulped in a deep breath. Who'd have thought she'd ever be this thankful to see Jake Dalton?

Chapter Three

"No problem that needs your help." The thug dropped his hold on Carolina's hand and backed up a step, but his eyes burned with fury. Jake sized him up. Physically fit, probably in his early thirties.

Jake figured he could still take him in a fair fight, but brawling in a parking lot wouldn't fix anything and was definitely not his style.

He turned to Carolina. "Was this man harassing you?"

"He's stalking Mildred."

"Having a conversation with my wife is not stalking."

Mildred hugged her arms around her chest, head down, looking more like a scared child facing an angry parent than a forceful woman. "I'm not your wife, Thad. We're divorced."

So the thug was Mildred's ex. That clarified

the situation a bit for Jake, even though it hadn't been Mildred the bully was manhandling.

The man reached a hand toward Mildred. "I just want to talk to you—in private."

Jake turned to Mildred. "Is that what you want?"

She shook her head and raised her eyes to Jake's, hers pleading when her gaze met his.

"I never meant to hurt you," Thad said, his tone considerably softer. "I love you. You know that. And you love me."

"You tried to kill her and almost succeeded," Carolina cut in, her words blistering. "She's through with you, so stay away from her or you'll be back in prison where you belong."

"Stay out of this, Carolina. You might own half of Texas, but you don't own Mildred and you sure as hell aren't going to order me around."

Jake struggled to contain his own anger as the situation became clearer still. The itch to punch Thad Caffey rode Jake hard.

He stepped toward Jake. "Mildred and Carolina are with me and you're through here. You have a problem with that, take it up with me now."

Thad glared at Mildred and then turned to Carolina. "So that's how it is. You got rid of me and now you've fixed my woman up with one of your rich rancher friends."

"One of my bulls would have been an improvement over you, Thad Caffey."

Thad beat his right fist into his left hand and ground it as if he were getting ready for a fight. Jake's muscles tensed. He'd never wanted to punch a guy more.

A second later, Thad turned and walked away without a backward glance. Jake watched him go, but his gut feeling was that this was far from being settled.

Jake lingered with the two women until Thad had sauntered over to an old mud-encrusted pickup truck with a rusted right fender and driven away.

"Good timing," Carolina said. "I'm not sure I could have taken him down if you hadn't shown up when you did. But I could have done some serious hair pulling and hopefully got in at least one knee to the groin."

"Ow. My bet's on you. But I'm glad I could intervene. Is there more to the story that I should know?"

"Thad is not a nice man," Mildred said.

"I got that."

"The four years in prison didn't make him any nicer," Carolina added.

"How long has he been out of prison?"

"Almost a week," Mildred said, "but last night was the first time he tried to contact me. I got a phone call from him at the hotel. I'm not sure how he found out I was here with Carolina. I don't know how far he would have pushed things today if you hadn't shown up when you did."

"Glad to help, but I seriously doubt you've seen the last of him. You should let his parole officer know he's stalking you."

"He doesn't have one. He served all his time."

"Then call your local sheriff."

"A great idea." Carolina took her car key from her handbag and pushed the unlock button. "We should get moving. Sara and Peg are probably already at the restaurant wondering what happened to us."

Jake glanced at the clouds that were rolling in. "I wouldn't dawdle over lunch," he suggested. "Weatherman may have been a little optimistic predicting the thunderstorms would hold off until evening."

He stepped past Carolina and opened the door for her. She brushed past him as she slid behind the wheel. Her skirt rode up her thighs, innocently provocative.

His senses reeled from an unexpected kick of sensual attraction. He was still feeling the effects long after they drove away.

Carolina Lambert was even more stunning in person than she was in her society page photos. Great body. Thick eyelashes. Sun-streaked hair that tumbled past her shoulders in soft, natural curls. Hazel eyes that sparked green when she was mad. Full, beautiful lips.

None of which changed the fact that she had manipulated R.J. into writing that bizarre, manipulative will, a will that she surely planned to work in her favor once R.J. was dead and gone and the family was released from his rules and regulations.

But a deal was a deal, even though he hadn't known it was her he was helping out this week. Carolina could do her thing. She'd have his wrangler's full cooperation.

But it was a large ranch. With luck, he wouldn't even have to see her again.

TWO HOURS LATER Carolina sped down the highway, barely paying attention to the conversation in the car as the four of them rolled down the last stretch of interstate before taking the exit for the Silver Spur Ranch.

The day had started with sunshine and promise. Now the sky was threatening. The cloud Thad Caffey had cast over the day was even gloomier.

If Jake hadn't walked up when he had, the situation might have turned violent. Just as frightening, Mildred might have gone with Thad in an effort to protect herself or Carolina from his rage.

Okay. Score one for Jake Dalton. She had to concede that he was not the complete cad she had figured him for. He'd been impressive in the parking lot, all the grit and virility a woman could ask for.

"I should have brought my rain slicker," Sara said from the backseat. "Looks as if it might start pouring any minute."

"It's not too late to turn around and try to reschedule the tour for first thing tomorrow morning," Carolina offered.

"We're almost there," Peg said. "Might as well see as much as we can today. If we need to check out more, we can always come back tomorrow and wade through the mud."

"The sexy ranch owner wouldn't have anything to do with your vote, would it?" Sara teased.

"No, but I can't say that I'd mind getting caught in the rain—or anywhere else with him. He is hot."

"Not to mention rich and single," Sara said.

"Better than all that, he seems like a really nice guy," Mildred said. "They're hard to come by."

It was one of the few times Mildred had joined the conversation since they left Austin. She had asked Carolina not to mention their run-in with Thad to the others, and Carolina had agreed that was for the best. Mildred didn't need a lot of questions thrown at her about her past experiences with her ex.

"How old do you think Jake is?" Peg asked.

"Maybe early fifties," Sara said. "What do you think, Carolina?"

"I'd say that's probably about right."

"I don't know," Peg said. "Those are not the biceps or butt of a middle-aged man."

"Good grief," Sara exclaimed. "What does age have to do with it? George Clooney, Kevin Costner, Colin Firth. My husband, Jess. All hunks past fifty."

"Doesn't just apply to men," Mildred added. "Case in point: Carolina. Remember the magazine article last year that declared her one of Texas's most beautiful and altruistic women?"

"A major exaggeration," Carolina said, as the others gave her a wahoo. "And for the record, I don't plan to spend a second of my time trying to impress Jake Dalton."

"Guess that leaves him to you and me, Mildred," Peg said, likely only half joking.

"Then he's all yours," Mildred said. "I like the single life."

Carolina turned at the entrance of the Silver Spur. The double gate of entwined metal links incorporated the images of two life-size rearing horses and the name of the ranch.

Sara stretched her neck to see more. "Wow. Impressive."

Carolina lowered her car window, pressed the call button that was mounted on a metal stand and looked into the lens of a security camera.

A few seconds later, a friendly female voice responded. "Hello. Welcome to the Silver Spur."

"Thanks. I'm Carolina Lambert, with the Saddle-Up project."

"Carolina Lambert," a female voice repeated, followed by a few seconds of silence. "The real Carolina Lambert?"

"I'm not sure who you're expecting, but I am real."

"I recognize you now. You know, from the pictures I see of you in the newspaper. Just last month you hosted that big fund-raiser for the children's hospital in Dallas."

"Yes, and thanks to a lot of very generous Texas donors, we surpassed our expectations. We're here to tour the ranch," she said. "Mr. Dalton said you'd be expecting us."

"He just said some ladies were driving out from Austin. He didn't say it was you. And I'm just blabbering on. Sorry. I'm Edna, Jake Dalton's housekeeper. You ladies just follow the main road back to the house and we'll have some proper introductions. I'll put the coffee on."

"Please don't go to any trouble for us."

"Coffee's no trouble. Can't miss the main house. Two story. White. Dark green shutters. Big covered porch."

"Is Mr. Dalton here this afternoon?"

"He's not back from the city yet, but Tilson can show you around. He's young, but one of the nicest wranglers you'll ever meet and he knows the spread like the back of his hand."

"I'm sure Tilson will be more than adequate."

The gate clicked, then swung open. Carolina shifted the gearshift into Drive and eased over the bumpy cattle gap. The gate creaked slightly as it automatically closed and locked behind them.

"Nice setup," Sara said. "I can't wait to see the house."

"Only thing missing is the boss man himself," Peg added. "Bummer."

So far, so good, Carolina decided as she stared at rolling pastures and the wooded areas that bordered them. The Silver Spur without Jake Dalton would work just fine.

"A SEVERE WEATHER watch will be in effect for Travis, Hays and Blanco counties from 4:00 p.m.

until 7:00 p.m. Be on the lookout for heavy rain and flash flooding in low-lying areas."

Jake turned down the volume on his truck radio and used the hands-free Bluetooth connection to call Lizzie. Weather anxiety skirted the other issues of the day as he waited for his daughter to answer her phone. When she didn't, he left a message.

"Storm is rolling in fast. I should be back to the ranch in about fifteen minutes. Hopefully you're there, as well, or at least somewhere safe. Call me as soon as you get this message."

When he broke the connection, he called his house. Edna answered on the fourth ring. After a quick hello he asked if the Saddle-Up team had defied the threatening storm and actually driven out to the ranch that afternoon.

"Yes, a couple of hours ago. I nearly passed out when I looked to see who was at the gate and Carolina Lambert was staring back at me."

He knew the feeling, only he hadn't been looking at a camera image. "I take it you pulled yourself together enough to let them in."

"Of course, but I can't believe you didn't tell me she was the Saddle-Up leader."

"I didn't know you were a Carolina Lambert groupie."

"Pshaw. I'm too old to be a groupie. But

she's famous. She attended a party at the White House once. I read that online."

"Guess that makes her a celebrity."

"She's not a bit stuck-up. All that money, and I swear she showed up here in a pair of Wranglers, worn cowboy boots and an ordinary white T-shirt. Just like regular people."

At least she'd changed out of that skirt that had inched up her thighs before she toured the ranch. He needed his wranglers working, not ogling.

"I hope the women left the ranch in time to make it back to Austin before the storm hits full force."

"They haven't left. They're still out with Tilson."

He swallowed a curse. Just what he needed. Carolina stuck at his house waiting out a storm. If they made it back to the house before it hit. "Did Tilson take them in one of the pickup trucks?"

"No. They wanted to go on horseback. I'm starting to worry about them, though. I haven't seen any lightning yet, but the thunder is sure rumbling and clouds are getting dark."

"Do you know where Lizzie is?"

"She's with Tilson and the ladies."

That did not sound like his daughter. "How did that happen?"

"Mrs. Lambert started asking her about the horses and the next thing I knew, Lizzie was headed to the horse barn with them. I haven't seen her since, so she must have decided to stay with the group."

Inspiring Lizzie to do anything that didn't include social media, texting or hanging out with her friends was a major accomplishment. If Lizzie was actually with them and hadn't slipped away from the ranch without mentioning it to Edna.

"I'll be home in a few minutes," he said. "Take care and stay inside. If you see Lizzie, tell her I said not to leave the house again."

"I'm sure that once she gets inside, she won't leave again in the storm."

Edna had more faith in Lizzie's judgment than he did. He broke the connection and gave his injured foreman a quick call. Granger answered on the first ring.

"How are the weather preparations going?" Jake asked.

"We're on top of things, even though I'm just able to man the phones. Winds are already gusting and blowing up whirlwinds of dust. Clouds are threatening to let loose with a deluge any minute now. Lanky's heading up to the big house to check on Edna, just in case she needs help with anything. He should be there any second."

"Sounds good. What about the livestock?"

"Got a couple of wranglers checking on the horses now. You know how spooked they get when a storm blows in. I had the cattle in pasture six moved to pasture five. Ground's higher there and will drain off a lot quicker if we get the rain they're forecasting. Feeding is taken care of."

"And the rest of the wranglers?"

"Told Fisher and Morgan to hightail it on home before the storm hits. The others are probably in the bunkhouse sipping whiskey and cooking up a bunch of fajitas by now."

"Edna tells me Tilson is still out with the ladies' tour group," Jake said.

"Just talked to him. They're on horseback and not five minutes from the big house. Lanky will help him take care of the horses after he drops off the ladies."

"That's what I needed to hear. I'm less than five minutes from the gate myself."

Streaks of lightning darted about the gray depths of the heavens as he broke the phone connection. A gust of wind made the truck shudder.

A big yellow dog ran the fence line just past the burned ruins of the old Baptist church. A shrieking murder of crows lined an electric line as if warning motorists they'd best get on home.

The first huge drops of rain began to pelt his windshield as he passed through the ranch gate. By the time he pulled into the three-car garage, the rain was falling in wind-driven sheets. He took the covered walkway to the back door.

Thankfully Tilson and the Saddle-Up group had made it back to the house, but not before the rain had hit. They were huddled in the kitchen, drenched to the skin. Carolina's gaze met his as he joined them, but it wasn't her eyes that brought him to instant attention.

Her firm breasts and puckered nipples were detailed beneath the clinging shirt. Arousal hit Jake so hard and fast it was dizzying.

He looked away quick, before the ache in his groin became a visible bulge.

He didn't even like the woman. What the hell was wrong with him?

Chapter Four

Tilson called his name and Jake jerked himself back to reality. "Sorry," he said. "I missed that."

"I was just apologizing for getting the ladies caught in the rain."

"Actually, it's our fault," Carolina corrected him. "We were so impressed with the view at Cotter's Canyon that we lingered too long."

Cotter's Canyon. *His* spot. More of a gulch than a canyon but special all the same. The place he went to get his head on straight. Now when he went there he'd most likely remember Carolina's nipples pressed against the white cotton.

Stunning even dripping wet. Sinfully sexy.

Texas was full of beautiful women. He needed to get out more, see something more intriguing than cows. A date every now and then couldn't hurt.

Edna stepped into the room, her arms filled

with fluffy white towels. She passed them around, and the ladies took them eagerly.

"I'd best get back to the horses," Tilson said.

"I'll help," Lanky said, "unless you want me to hang around longer, boss man."

"No. You and Tilson just take care of the horses. Move quickly and take cover if need be. There are some extra ponchos on hooks in the garage," Jake said. "Grab a couple."

"Too late now. Besides, a little rain never hurt a cowboy," Tilson said. "Mighty sorry for letting our guests get caught in the downpour, though."

Unwittingly Jake's gaze swept back to Carolina. She dabbed her face before wrapping long locks of dripping hair between folds of the thick terry.

"Where's Lizzie?" Jake asked, coming to his senses to realize she was missing from the group.

"Headed straight to her room to get out of her wet clothes," Edna said.

"You have a lovely daughter," Carolina said.

"Really fun to be around," Peg added.

"Thank you." Obviously they'd seen the side of Lizzie she seldom shared with him anymore.

"We're puddling your floors," Carolina said, looking down. "If you'll get me a mop, I'll clean up our mess."

"Guests don't mop," Edna said quickly. "I'm more worried about the four of you standing around in those wet clothes. Why don't I show you to guest rooms and gather some robes? You can change into them and I'll toss your wet clothes into the dryer. They'll be ready for you to put back on in no time."

All four of the women voiced their approval of that.

Jake walked over to the counter to start a pot of coffee while the women now draped in thirsty towels followed Edna to retrieve the robes. As usual, Edna was way ahead of him. The pot was full.

He was halfway through a mug of hot brew when Lizzie padded barefoot into the kitchen. Her long auburn hair was turbaned in a light blue towel. Her too-skimpy white denim shorts rode low on her hips. A blue cropped top showed far too much skin for his liking.

As tempted as he was to send her back to her room for something more suitable for guests, he decided to let it ride this time.

"Where did everyone go?" she asked.

"To change into robes so that Edna could dry their clothes."

"I'll go see if I can help." She headed for the hallway.

"Lizzie."

She stopped and turned toward him with a roll of her eyes. "What did I do now?"

"Nothing. I appreciate you helping out today. It was a…" He searched for the right words.

"Decent thing to do. I get it, Dad. Don't sound so shocked. I'm not completely heathen."

"I was simply saying thanks."

"Yeah." She nodded and left the room.

He couldn't even pull off being appreciative and make it work with her anymore. How had the gulf between him and his daughter ever grown so wide?

Jake checked the weather radar on his phone. The entire county was getting hit, but the worst was north of them, toward Austin. He stamped to the mudroom, grabbed the mop from the closet and went to work on the floor.

"Keep that up and you'll scrub the finish off the tiles," Edna said, rejoining him in the kitchen a few minutes later.

He looked down. The floor was completely dry. He eased his grip on the mop handle as lightning zigzagged across the sky, followed by a clap of thunder that shook the windows.

"Keeps storming like this and a few of those low-lying roads are sure to flood," Edna said.

"Lucky we have plenty of spare bedrooms if the ladies need to stay over."

A sleepover with Carolina was exactly what he didn't need. "Storm will likely pass in a couple of hours."

"Might. Might not. I'll take some chicken out of the freezer just in case. It can be thawing while I wash their clothes."

"What happened to the plan to just throw them in the dryer for a few minutes?"

"The hems of the jeans were muddy and everything smelled of wet horseflesh."

"Nothing wrong with that. This is a ranch."

"We don't have to smell like the horses. Besides, it's not as if they have to get dressed immediately. They can't set off for Austin in this storm. I told them to slip out of everything and put the laundry outside the door. I'll pick their soiled clothes up in a few minutes and toss them in the washer while they just make themselves at home."

"You are definitely getting into this."

"Do you blame me? It's not every day we have someone like Carolina Lambert in the house."

"Now you're knocking my friends."

"You know what I mean. She's exciting and so interesting. Her friends are nice, too. Even Lizzie is enjoying herself, in case you haven't noticed."

He'd noticed. He'd dated a few times since Gloria's death. None of the women had made anywhere near the impression Carolina was making.

"Did you know that Carolina is a widow with three adult sons and four grandchildren?" Edna asked.

"I've heard that."

"She doesn't look nearly old enough to have grown sons or be a grandmother."

He couldn't argue with that.

"Her son Durk is the CEO of the family oil business and her other two sons, Damien and Tague, manage the Bent Pine Ranch."

"You are just chock-full of information today."

"I like to know about the people I'll be entertaining for the next few days."

"Whoa. We are not entertaining them. They're using our facilities and our horses, but we're not involved. It's totally their show. Keep that in mind."

"That doesn't mean I can't be hospitable. You need to do the same. You never know. You might just find some chemistry with one of our guests."

"I'm not looking for chemistry."

"It might find you anyway if you'd stop being so contrary." Edna pulled a package of chicken from the freezer. "I settled the ladies into all four of our guest suites. Made sure they had plenty of that good-smelling soap, shampoo, and fresh towels and washcloths, too."

Great. So now Carolina Lambert was taking a hot shower under his roof. Naked. He swallowed hard, determined to keep his arousal level at low-key. He didn't like the woman, and with good reason. Why couldn't his manly urges get that?

"Just remember you're bringing all this extra work on yourself, Edna. Don't blame me if your good intentions turn into more than you bargained for. In the meantime, I'll be in my office if you need me—getting some work done while we still have power."

"Good thinking. I'll put out some candles and the oil lamps. Never know when the electricity will go out."

His office was down the hall on the first floor, far away from all the guest rooms—except one, which was only a few steps from his office. With his luck, Carolina was probably stripping out of her clothes in that one right now.

CAROLINA STARED OUT the window and into a torrent of rain. She should be back in her hotel room in Austin. But here she was, standing in one of Jake Dalton's guest rooms, no longer dripping, but with her damp clothes clinging to her like a clammy second skin. She looked away from the storm and glanced around the room.

A king-size bed topped with a dark green comforter was piled high with pillows. A small antique desk held a cup of pens, some note paper and several hardcover novels displayed between beautifully sculptured horse-head bookends. A floor mirror in a beautiful oak stand adorned a far corner.

The walls were painted a pale green and decorated with framed photographs of Texas landscapes, at least two of which she was certain had been taken on the Silver Spur. She recognized the magnificent views from this afternoon's ride.

A wooden rocker next to the window with a flowered cushion and a knitted afghan thrown over its arm looked cozy and inviting.

Difficult to imagine the calming decor was the rugged rancher's doing. But then, she had to admit, she actually knew little about the man other than his coldhearted stubbornness where R.J. was concerned.

Thinking about the brief phone conversation she'd shared with him a few days back still left her seething. She couldn't understand anyone unwilling to bend a little for a dying parent—even if R.J. had been a rotten father.

She dropped the towel she was wearing sarong-style over her wet clothes and caught a glimpse of herself in the full-length mirror. She grimaced. Her wet, curly locks and runny mascara gave new meaning to the drowned-rat cliché. Her gaze fell lower.

Ohmigod. She could see every pucker of her nipples beneath the damp cotton of her shirt. The others' shirts had been just as wet—but not white. They'd clung, but she hadn't noticed that you could see right through them.

No wonder Jake had stared so hard. She might as well have stripped off her shirt.

Her cheeks burned. How was she going to face the guy again? Not without a bit of embarrassment, that was for sure. As if things weren't awkward enough between them.

No use to dwell on it now. There was no changing the facts. She undressed quickly, peeling off everything, including her bra and panties. Then she dropped the wet clothing outside her door as Edna had instructed.

She wondered if Jake knew what a jewel of a housekeeper he had in Edna. Hopefully he was a lot more considerate to her than he was to R.J.

Carolina headed to the bathroom, took a

quick shower to shed the odor of horseflesh and then used a fresh towel to buff her naked body.

The overhead light flickered a couple of times but didn't go out as she padded back into the bedroom. She wrapped herself in the soft robe, though she had no intention of going back to the den until she was fully dressed.

She threw back the coverlet and slid between the sheets. It was like sinking into a cloud. The serenity lasted only until thoughts of the morning encounter with Thad Caffey returned to haunt her.

Mildred had thought her life with him was behind her. Clearly, Thad did not share that sentiment. But how far would he go to get her back?

How sad for Mildred that her marriage had deteriorated into fear and danger. Yet she must have cared deeply for Thad at one time, before the love changed to fear and heartbreak. Before she saw the man she'd vowed to share her life with as the monster he really was.

Carolina had difficulty comprehending that kind of relationship. Her life with Hugh had been loving and exciting. If anything he'd been overly protective of her. A man's man, all the way. He'd been her world, and she'd never known fear of anything or anyone when he was around.

The familiar ache set in again. As busy as her life was, as much as she loved her family, her heart still longed for the relationship she'd shared with Hugh.

Having known that kind of love, she could never settle for anything less. She had no illusions that she'd ever find love like that again.

Chapter Five

The pain was blinding, as if someone were hammering nails into his skull. Not a new pain, but one that had become excruciatingly more familiar since the day he'd been sentenced to four agonizing years in prison.

He recognized the torture for what it was, knew the only real release would come when he was back in control. When he could feel the sweet release of revenge.

He'd had four years to plan the payback. Nights of trying to fall asleep to the sounds of rants from half-insane inmates and the scratching of rats scurrying in and out of his stinking cell. Days of staring at bars and marching to the barking orders of guards whom he longed to twist apart like rotten fruit.

Four years of torture. It was time for action. The plan was all in place. The clock was clicking inside the very marrow of his bones.

He picked up the bottle of beer from the bar in front of him, took the last gulp and signaled to the waitress to bring him another.

Before she could, a platinum blonde wearing a low-cut top and inches of thick makeup got up from her stool a few down from his and walked over.

"Want some company? Looks like the rain is going to be with us for a while."

He didn't want company, but he shrugged and she obviously took that for a yes. She slid onto the stool next to his.

"I hate stormy Mondays."

"Yeah," he muttered. In prison a man lost track of the days. They came and went in a steady stream of monotonous boredom, seeing the same people, eating the same lousy food, staring at the same dull walls.

"You married?" she asked.

"Yeah. My wife is out screwing some wealthy rancher. Is that what you're looking for, too? I figure you're just another slut looking for some man to pay for your drinks and maybe get in your pants."

"You're crazy, you know that? A freakin' nutcase." She stood and walked away.

The waitress put his bottle of beer in front of him without saying a word. He threw a few bills on the bar, gulped down his beer, then got up and walked out of the nearly empty bar.

The rain needled his skin. He kept walking. The hammering grew worse. If he didn't let off some steam soon, he'd explode.

Chapter Six

Carolina was curled up beneath the comforter, trying to concentrate on a suspense novel she'd taken from the antique desk. She looked up at a light tap on her door.

She glanced at her watch. Almost five. "Come in."

Peg did, still in her robe and barefoot, since their boots probably wouldn't be dry for hours. Yet her hair was dry and shiny, makeup meticulously applied.

"Laundry's done." She handed Carolina her jeans, shirt, socks and undies.

"You even folded them. Thanks."

"Actually, Edna folded them. She wouldn't let me or Sara near the laundry room."

"We'll have to think of something nice to do for her after this week," Carolina said. "Have you seen Mildred?"

"Not yet, but Edna is taking her dry clothes

to her now. She would have delivered yours, but she was afraid of waking you. She thinks you're royalty."

"That's what happens when you make the society page."

They both laughed. "I told Edna you're a workaholic and were probably in here finalizing and double-checking everything for the Saddle-Up training."

"You know me too well," Carolina answered, sidestepping the truth.

Working would have been far more productive than vacillating between concerns about what Thad Caffey might try next and trying to figure out how she could totally manage to avoid Jake Dalton, especially after her wet T-shirt display.

"Edna suggested we meet back in the den for cocktails or a glass of wine once we're dressed."

"I'll join you, but no alcohol for me. I still have to drive back to Austin tonight."

"If the roads are passable. That was a deluge for about an hour."

Peg shut the door behind her as she left. Carolina slid off the side of the bed and padded over to the window.

The wind had stopped howling, the thunder had faded into the distance and the driving rain no longer swept the windows in sheets. Only a light mist and a blanket of dark clouds re-mained—the clouds a lingering threat that the weather might not be through with them yet.

Carolina dressed hurriedly, finished drying her hair and put on a tinge of lipstick before heading back to the den. She heard the laughter as soon as she started down the hallway.

"Thought you'd abandoned us," Mildred said when Carolina rearranged a couple of throw pillows and took a seat on the end of a deep brown leather sofa.

"I had some paperwork to do."

Lizzie perched on the arm of the other end of the sofa. "Those camps must be a lot of work, but I bet those kids love it—or do some of them hate it?"

"Some do when they first arrive," Carolina admitted. "But we usually convert them long before the month is over. The horses win their hearts."

"I know. When I got my first very own colt, I even slept in the horse barn a few nights. Do you teach Western saddle riding?"

"Absolutely," Carolina said. "We do the whole cowgirl experience. Riding, some minimal rop-ing, sampling every kind of taco you can imag-ine and singing songs around the campfire. Of course they have to learn to clean stables and take care of the horses, too."

"Naturally. So, do you get out with the kids yourself or just sponsor the camps and the training?"

"I'm hands-on," Carolina said, "especially for the fun activities."

"She's out there every day, all day," Mildred said. "Works harder than any of us."

"Awesomesauce," Lizzie said. "The way Edna talks, you're like a queen or something."

"Those were not my exact words," Edna denied, untying and pulling off her apron as she joined them in the den. "But I'm impressed myself that you're out there with the kids getting all hot and sweaty."

Peg joined them in the den. "Looks like the gang's all here except for the boss man himself. Where did your father disappear to, Lizzie?"

Lizzie shrugged. "Who knows? He's always doing something on the ranch. Some days we hardly see him."

"Running a ranch is hard work," Edna reminded her. "Does anyone mind if I turn on the TV? I'd like to catch the early-evening news, see what they have to say about that storm that blew through here like a wailing banshee."

Of course, no one objected.

They tuned in just in time to be reminded that a little pill could guarantee them a perfect sex life at any moment with no preparation. It had been years since Carolina had given much thought to a sex life.

The top news story of the night was the storm. The screen switched to a live shot of a male reporter in a dark blue wind jacket standing in water up to his knees. The running print dialogue below the images warned of flash flooding in low-lying areas in and around Austin.

"Looks like Austin got the brunt of it," Peg said as images of flooded streets, overflowing drainage ditches and cars stranded on the highway were shown in rapid succession.

"Good thing we didn't hang around there all afternoon," Mildred said.

"Or get out on the road during the storm," Sara added as the images and narrative skipped to the report of a six-car pileup on the interstate. "We could have been stuck out there for hours if we'd been behind that."

"Numerous fender benders and stalled cars have basically shut down the interstates in all directions around Austin," the reporter continued. "Stay off the roads unless it's absolutely necessary, but if you must venture out, watch out for rising water."

"That settles it," Edna said. "It is definitely not safe or sane for you ladies to drive back to Austin tonight. There's plenty of room for all four of you to stay right here."

"Makes sense for Mildred and Carolina," Sara agreed. "I definitely wouldn't risk flooding out Carolina's sports car if I were her. But our ranch is less than a half hour from here. My hubby will come pick up Peg and me in his four-wheel-drive pickup truck."

"Staying here works for me," Mildred said.

It definitely did not work for Carolina. Things were awkward enough as they were without adding a sleepover with Jake to the mix. "Thanks for the offer, Edna, but I'm sure the roads will be safe for travel again in a couple of hours."

Conversation stopped as the back door opened, followed by heavy footsteps. A few seconds later, Jake joined them in the den.

Jake's six-foot-plus frame and commanding demeanor dominated the scene even before he said a word.

"Any storm problems?" Edna asked.

"Some of the horses needed a bit of calming down, as usual, but no wind damage that I noticed except for a couple of limbs down in that stretch of pines along the creek."

"Did you check the entire ranch?" Peg asked.

"Not enough time for that, but we've been through enough storms to know where floods and the wind usually do their damage."

Edna straightened the skirt of her blue-flowered housedress. "You should have seen the pictures of the flooding in Austin."

"Too much rain or not enough. That's Texas."

"I invited the ladies to spend the night," Edna said. "No use for them to risk facing a flash-flooding situation."

For the first time since he entered the room, Jake turned and looked directly at Carolina, his dark eyes peering into hers. Her chest grew tight.

"If you want to stay, there's room."

That wasn't exactly what she'd call an eager agreement.

"We've already been far too intrusive in your lives," Carolina said. "I'm sure the roads will clear up enough that we can get back to our hotel tonight."

"Suit yourself, but the offer stands. Now if you ladies will excuse me, I need to make a few phone calls." He started toward the hallway, then stopped and turned back to face Carolina. "If you had no problems with Tilson today, I'll assign him to assist you in any way he can during the training session. If you need other wranglers, he can line them up."

She wondered if that offer was to make up for Jake's less than enthusiastic offer of hospitality.

Even so, she could use the help. "I appreciate that, and I'm sure Tilson will do fine."

"Does that mean you're neglecting us?" Peg asked, her voice bordering on outright seduction.

"I'll be around if you need me, but I'll do my best to stay out of your way." He stopped next to Lizzie and put a hand on her shoulder. "Don't even think about leaving the house tonight."

"Wasn't planning to."

"I'd better get back in the kitchen and get started on those chicken enchiladas," Edna said.

"Please don't go to any extra trouble for us."

"No trouble at all. Nothing more fun than having a full table to cook for. Is dinner at seven okay?"

"Perfect," they said in unison.

"I'll give Edna a hand," Mildred said, following the housekeeper to the kitchen.

"You know, Lizzie, I don't think your dad's as excited as Edna about having a houseful of women around," Sara said. "Not that I blame him, since he doesn't even know us."

"No. That's just how he is," Lizzie said. "He doesn't get excited about much. But if he didn't want you here, you'd know it."

Lizzie's cell phone rang. She grabbed it and answered quickly, "What's up?"

She left the room before she said more, but it was clear from her suddenly strained expression that the phone call was upsetting.

Lizzie was vivacious and smart, but Carolina had a feeling she was also as complex and troubled as many of the youngsters who'd show up for the Saddle-Up summer-camp program.

Now that she thought about it, Lizzie, with her knowledge and love of horses and riding, would be a perfect junior volunteer for the session on Sara's ranch. Not only would the participants learn from her, but the interaction with young teens so much less fortunate than herself might do Lizzie some good, as well.

Her involvement would require Lizzie's willingness and Jake's permission. The latter might be the more difficult to obtain, but worth a shot.

Determined to face the issue before she changed her mind, she went off in search of Jake. It didn't take long to find him. He was at a wide wooden desk in his home office, staring at a table of figures on the computer screen. She tapped lightly on the open door.

He looked up. "Come in."

"Is this a bad time?"

"No. Can I help you with something?"

"Hopefully. It's about Lizzie."

His brow furrowed. "What about her?"

"She's a really nice kid. Smart and great with horses, too."

"Thank you."

"She's got a lot going for her, but she's—"

"Look, Mrs. Lambert, if you're here to tell me that she has a problem with me, don't bother. I'm quite aware. It's not for lack of trying on my part. It's just…"

"Carolina."

He frowned. "What?"

"You can call me Carolina. And I'm not here to criticize but to ask a favor of sorts. I'd appreciate it if you'd hear me out before you say no."

"Go ahead."

"I'd like your permission to invite Lizzie to be one of our junior counselors this summer. She has so much to offer, and I think it might even be good for her."

"Exactly what would that involve?"

"One month of working with the underprivileged campers on Sara and Jess's ranch. It would be voluntary, but she could stay on site with the other camp counselors so she wouldn't have to be on the highway driving back and forth."

"Have you mentioned this to Lizzie?"

"No. I wanted to clear it with you first."

Jake swiveled his chair so that he was facing Carolina. Concern etched his face. "If you can persuade my daughter to give up sleeping until noon and then spending the rest of the day either texting or hanging out with her friends, I'd say you're a miracle worker."

"I'll take that as a yes."

"Definitely. Go for it. You do the asking. If it comes from me, the answer would be an unqualified no."

Perhaps if you set a better example with the way you treated your own father.

Those were the words Carolina wanted to toss back at him. She bit them back. Lizzie needed her father, and if they didn't find a way to connect soon, they might never find it.

"Carolina. I've been looking all over for you."

She looked up as Mildred rushed into the room, her face a pasty white. "What's wrong?"

"Thad. He's not giving up."

Chapter Seven

Jake was not surprised. He had sat out the storm at ranch headquarters, checking the internet for anything he could find about the arrest and trial that led to Caffey's conviction.

There hadn't been much. As rotten a crime as spousal abuse was, it didn't get a lot of press unless either the perpetrator or the victim was a celebrity.

The sketchy details indicated that Thad had abused Mildred throughout their three years of marriage in what the prosecutor described as mental and physical torture.

Slugging her for simple mistakes like scorching his shirt when she was ironing it or not scrubbing the kitchen floor as clean as he wanted it. Always hitting her somewhere the bruises could be hidden beneath her clothes.

On other occasions, he wouldn't tell her what she'd done wrong but would lock her in a room for days with only tepid water to drink. And yet she'd stayed with him. Now he was back again.

"I can't believe he has the gall to contact you," Carolina said, "much less to keep harassing you. On second thought, knowing Thad, of course he had the gall. What did he say?"

"Not much. It was a text this time." She handed the phone to Carolina, who read the brief message aloud.

"'Waiting for you at the hotel. Need to talk— alone. Miss my wife.'"

"He must have found out where we're staying," Mildred said.

"Good. Let him wait for us. The police will know where to arrest him for stalking you."

Jake doubted a text asking to talk to an ex-wife was grounds for arrest. Unless... "Is Caffey under any legal orders to stay away from you?"

"No," Mildred admitted. "I didn't ask for that, never dreamed I'd need it. He wrote me several times the first year, telling me that I'd turned on him and he never wanted to see me again."

"Has he written since the first year?"

"Only once, when the divorce became final. He wrote me a blistering three-page letter reminding me of all he'd done for me and saying what a thankless bitch I was. Mostly he railed on Carolina, accusing her of turning me against him."

"Naturally he didn't take any responsibility for his actions," Carolina said.

"After that, I never heard from him again," Mildred continued. "I only knew he was out of prison because Sheriff Garcia called me. He's our local sheriff and the one who arrested Thad the night he almost killed me."

"I know Garcia. Good man," Jake said, though he'd only met the sheriff once and that had been a couple of years back.

Jake hadn't actually been invited into this discussion, but having it take place in his home office should give him some rights. Besides, neither Carolina nor Mildred seemed to resent his input.

"How long did you say Caffey's been out of prison?" he asked.

"Five days to be exact."

"And last night was the first time he's tried to contact you?"

"Yes. I'm so sorry about this. I never would have come to the training program if I'd known he was going to start trouble."

"Nonsense and don't apologize," Carolina insisted. "You've done nothing wrong. Thad is the one who's out of order."

Jake agreed, but in spite of her bluster, Carolina was not the one to take on a man who fell into rage the way Caffey did.

"I think you should give Sheriff Garcia a call," Jake said. "Let him know what's going on and see what he advises. If he thinks a restraining order is called for, I'm sure he can expedite it. Then if your ex harasses you, Mildred, there's grounds for an arrest."

"Good idea," Carolina agreed.

Mildred looked uncertain. "That's only going to upset him more. Maybe I should try talking to Thad first."

Jake figured Mildred was falling back into her old ways of trying to smooth things over with Thad. "I wouldn't recommend that."

"Giving in to Thad will do nothing but encourage him," Carolina said.

"I guess you're right."

Jake was certain Carolina was right, but that still left Caffey waiting for them back in Austin. Another confrontation. A better-than-average chance that Caffey would lose his temper again.

Not going to happen on Jake's watch. He was about to invite a heap of complications into his life, but he couldn't see any way around it.

Jake stood and walked to the front of his desk, then nonchalantly leaned his backside against it. "You might want to rethink driving back into Austin tonight."

"That won't be necessary," Carolina assured him. "I'll alert hotel security. They'll see that there's no trouble."

"What if they can't?" Mildred asked. "What if Thad outsmarts them like he always fools everyone?" She wrung her hands. "I'd feel better if we stayed here—just for tonight."

"Plenty of room," Jake said. "Won't put anyone out."

Carolina's lips pressed together, as if spending the night at the Silver Spur was a major concession. Her resentment toward him was no secret, but she could show a little appreciation. He wasn't the monster forcing the change of plans.

Finally, she looked up and met his gaze. "If you're sure you're comfortable with us here?"

He was anything but comfortable with Carolina sleeping under his roof, but that was a matter between him and his libido. It would help if she weren't so damned attractive when she was playing Mama Bear.

"So what do I do about the text?" Mildred asked.

"Nothing," Jake said. "Don't answer or delete unless the sheriff instructs you to."

"Thanks. After four years of not dealing with Thad, I had forgotten how much he frightens me. But today in the parking lot and then tonight when I read his text, I got that same nauseating feeling in my stomach that I had every day and night of living with him. Never knowing which Thad would come home at night—the loving husband or the devil."

Carolina put a hand around Mildred's shoulder. "You don't ever have to go back to that again."

"I hope you're right. I'll go call the sheriff now. The sooner I can get the restraining order started, the better." She turned to go. "Thank you so much for letting us stay here, Mr. Dalton. I'm sure I'll sleep much better knowing Thad won't come busting into my room any second."

"Glad to help, and call me Jake."

"Okay, Jake."

Carolina rocked on the heels of her stockinged feet as Mildred disappeared into the hallway. "Thanks, but you really didn't have to do that," she said.

"It's just a bed for a night, Carolina. It's not that big a deal."

"Isn't it? I saw your face this morning when you realized I was the one you had to put up with for almost a week. You were anything but pleased."

"I was surprised, but not bothered at all by your being here."

Carolina was a woman used to getting what she wanted. Nothing daunted Carolina Lambert.

Best not to let her know that she daunted him, especially now that she'd be sleeping under his roof.

THE EVENING DRAGGED by for Carolina, but there were no more awkward conversations between her and Jake. He made an excuse to skip out on dinner and didn't show up again until Jess arrived to pick up Sara and Peg.

Once they were gone, she excused herself and made her way back to the comfortable guest room, one just steps away from his office.

When she reached the room, she threw back the coverlet, sat on the bed and pulled off the thick socks she'd worn in lieu of wet boots or going barefoot. Fatigue, mental as much as physical, set in so powerfully that the tasks of undressing and washing her face seemed monumental. She stretched out on the bed fully clothed.

A little more than twenty-four hours after their arrival in Austin with high expectations and excitement, everything had gone wrong. She had Thad Caffey to thank for that. He was a beast of a man who'd intimidated and terrorized Mildred for years while pretending to love her. He apparently planned to pick up where he'd left off the night he was arrested.

No wonder he struck such fear in Mildred.

But the last person she'd expected to come to the rescue was Jake Dalton. She'd had him all figured out before she met him. Arrogant. Coldhearted. No respect for the feelings of his dying father.

So exactly how was she supposed to integrate that with the man who was so quick to come to the rescue tonight? Not that the tension between them had decreased. If anything, it was stronger, almost palpable.

She could neither understand nor deny that he had a dizzying effect on her.

A light tap at the door interrupted the troubling thoughts. Mildred poked her head in. "Mind if I come in?"

"Of course not. Is something wrong?"

"No, but I still haven't heard back from Sheriff Garcia. Maybe he didn't get my message. Do you think I should call again?"

"If you want to, but he works crazy hours, depending on what's going on in the area."

"I know. I just keep thinking of Thad in Austin, waiting on me to get there and getting madder by the second."

"We stayed here so you can get a good night's sleep."

"I know, and I do feel safer than I would back

at the hotel. Even you have to admit, Jake has been a lifesaver today."

"I wouldn't go that far, but he's come through for us."

"I think he likes you."

"I think he's tolerating me—admittedly more than he's doing with R.J."

Carolina was grateful when Mildred's phone rang and killed the subject at hand.

Mildred yanked the phone from the pocket of a white chenille robe. "It's Sheriff Garcia."

Carolina pulled her legs into bed with her and sat cross-legged, her back propped against a stack of pillows, as she listened to Mildred's side of the conversation. After about ten minutes of rehashing the latest developments, she handed the phone to Carolina.

"The sheriff wants to talk to you."

Carolina took the phone and exchanged a greeting. The sheriff wasted no time in getting down to business.

"I know you always mean well, Carolina, trying to solve everybody's problems, but don't go thinking you can handle Thad Caffey the way you do one of your ornery quarter horses."

"I have no intention of dealing with Thad. That's why Mildred called you."

"Good that you did. Based on Thad's history, there will be no trouble getting a restraining order. If Thad disobeys it, I can immediately put out a warrant for his arrest."

"That's what we're hoping for."

"Surprised the heck out of me when Mildred told me where you're staying for the rest of the week. When did you and Jake Dalton get to be such good buddies?"

"We didn't. It's a long story, but we'll be using his ranch for a Saddle-Up training session."

"Mighty convenient. Does that mean he and R.J. mended fences?"

"No."

"Then you must have had some sweet change of heart."

"No." It never failed to amaze her how much everyone in the small town of Oak Grove knew about her business. Nonetheless she wasn't feeding the gossip gristmill with the sheriff.

"Anyway, long as you stay at the Silver Spur Ranch, I won't be worrying about you. You're as safe on the ranch with Jake Dalton as you'd be with me or one of my deputies."

"Do you know Jake?"

"Met him once when I had to question a guy who was working for him. Good rancher. No nonsense."

"I'm glad you approve of our living arrangements." Not that she was planning to stay at the

Silver Spur on a twenty-four-hour basis until Sunday afternoon, though it might be wise for Mildred to stay here.

A matter they could discuss in the morning.

"What do your sons have to say about this?" Garcia asked.

"I haven't talked to them about it."

"Don't you think you should?"

"Mildred's ex showed up and wants to talk to her. That doesn't seem like something I should pull them into. Besides, Durk and his wife are at an energy conference in Saudi Arabia this week. Damien and his family are spending a couple of weeks at the family fishing cabin in Colorado. Which means Tague is left to run the ranch by himself."

"Tague might be busy, but he'd want to know what's going on."

"He'd worry and there's no reason for that."

They wrapped up the conversation quickly and broke the connection. Mildred seemed much calmer now that she'd actually talked to the sheriff and they had a plan. Within minutes, she said good-night and returned to her room.

Carolina stripped out of her clothes and climbed naked beneath the crisp sheets. It had been a long, stressful day. She was bone tired. Still, when she turned off the light and closed her eyes, she saw Jake Dalton. Strong. Virile. Piercing eyes the color of dark chocolate.

A heated shimmer ran through her. She punched her pillow and forced the image from her mind.

Still, sleep was a long time in coming.

GARCIA LEANED BACK in his office chair, kicked out of his worn work boots and propped his aching feet on his desk. He ought to turn over more work to his deputies and quit putting in these ten-hour days.

Hell, a man his age should be retired. Trouble was, puttering around an empty house got boring real quick. And there were just so many old John Wayne movies a man could watch.

It wasn't like the old days, though. Then men like Thad Caffey were few and far between. Now they seemed to multiply like weeds in a pea patch. These days a lawman put his life on the line every time he approached a suspect or stopped a car for speeding.

Never understood how a nice girl like Mildred got mixed up with a thug like Caffey. Lucky for her that Carolina had taken her under her wing. Carolina could never turn down a worthy cause.

Garcia had known Carolina ever since Hugh Lambert married her and brought her back to the Bent Pine Ranch. At the time, she'd been the most beautiful woman Garcia had ever seen. It figured a man like Hugh would get her. Rich, powerful, charismatic and tough. A man's man.

That had been the first time Garcia had seriously lusted for another man's wife. He'd never stopped. But then half the men in the county were at least halfway in love with Carolina. Stunning looks. A heart of gold. An easy smile. There was nothing not to love.

Reaching into his shirt pocket, Garcia pulled out a toothpick, removed it from its cellophane wrapper and stuck it between his teeth. Chewing the strip of wood was a bad habit he'd picked up two years ago at the doctor's orders to replace an even worse habit.

He still missed his cigars. Never more than times like this when a gnawing uneasiness coated the lining of his stomach with acid.

He stared at the wall in front of him, but his mind's eye returned to the courtroom the day Thad Caffey was sentenced. There hadn't been a sign of remorse on his face. Instead his eyes had burned with rage when he stared straight at Carolina Lambert.

Mildred was likely not the only woman in danger from a deranged lunatic. Garcia needed to make one more phone call tonight.

Chapter Eight

The dull gray of predawn sneaked through the slats of the blinds. Jake rolled over and checked the time. Ten after five. His body protested the movement, craving more than the few hours of restless sleep it had been given. He could bury his head in the pillow, but chances were slim he'd fall back asleep even if he stayed in bed.

Resigned, he threw his legs over the side of the bed and walked to the window. The storm had blown over, leaving the land to soak up the water for the long, hot summer to follow. The storm of complications had only just begun.

Last night's conversation with Sheriff Garcia replayed in his mind. The sheriff's call had only verified what Jake had already surmised from his brief encounter with Caffey and what he'd read about the trial.

Thad Caffey was a man given to rage before he went to prison. There was no reliable way to judge what he might be capable of now. The restraining order was the sensible next step, but it might send him over the edge. And if it did, the wife he was trying to win back would not necessarily be his first intended victim.

Jake pulled a pair of worn jeans from his closet and wiggled into them. The house was quiet and likely would be for another hour or two.

He'd get a head start on things, drive over to ranch headquarters and make some changes to the day's wrangler assignments. Assign a couple of guys to keep an eye on things around the house, though even Garcia had agreed it was extremely doubtful Caffey would show up here.

Cowards who beat up women didn't voluntarily tangle with armed wranglers, especially considering how fast Caffey had backed away yesterday when Jake interrupted his confrontation with the ladies.

Nonetheless, it always paid to be prepared.

But first, Jake needed a shot of caffeine.

He padded down the hallway in his bare feet. He paused at Lizzie's doorway, the familiar ache hitting again. He'd failed her as a father, was clueless as to how to bridge the gap that had grown between them.

Yet Carolina had shown up on the scene and bonded in one afternoon. Not only had she won

Lizzie over, but she had the usually wary Edna more excited than he'd seen her in eons.

Far more surprising, she'd aroused him to the point it was embarrassing. Strange and scary powers, the beautiful rancher possessed.

His nostrils captured their first whiff of fresh-brewed coffee at the staircase landing. Evidently Edna was too excited over their famous guest to sleep and had beaten the sun up this morning.

He stopped abruptly at the kitchen door. It wasn't Edna but Carolina who stood in half shadows, facing the window. Her hair was pinned on top of her head, loose tendrils floating down the back of her neck and dancing along the collar of the pale blue robe. In his kitchen at daybreak, sucking up all the oxygen in the room.

He swallowed a curse as physical reactions he didn't understand and couldn't control rocked his body. He struggled to fill his lungs enough that he could make a stab at speaking intelligently.

"You're up early." Not a particularly brilliant opener.

Carolina startled at his voice and spun around to face him.

"Sorry," he muttered. "I didn't mean to frighten you."

"I didn't hear you walk up. Guess I was too lost in my thoughts."

"I trust they weren't all bad."

"They could have been better. Thad Caffey has definitely put a damper on my enthusiasm. I tossed and turned much of the night."

Jake's imagination jumped back into play. Images of her kicking off the sheets, her body stretched out across the bed, flew to his mind. Testosterone shot through his veins, accompanied by a jolt of protective urges.

Those were the urges he needed to heed. There was too much at risk to let his libido call the shots.

"Mind if I join you in a cup of coffee?" he asked.

"Why don't I take mine back to the bedroom and leave your kitchen to you?"

"I'd rather you stay for a few minutes. We need to talk."

The four scariest words in the English language. Her eyes were shadowed with dread at what might come next.

FEELING UNEASY AND INTRUSIVE, Carolina studied Jake as he filled a mug with the hot brew. He might want to talk, but she was pretty sure he hadn't expected to run into her in his kitchen this early in the morning.

His hair was mussed from sleep, one dark lock falling over his forehead. His bare chest revealed swirls of even darker hair that narrowed where they disappeared into the unsnapped waistband of his jeans.

She looked away quickly as a slow burn snaked along her nerve endings. It was hard not to be aware of a man who wore his virility like a second skin, especially in a setting as intimate as this one.

She took a deep breath and pulled the tie tighter on the borrowed robe. Next time she came downstairs this early…

Whoa. What was she thinking? There would be no next time. No matter what Mildred decided, Carolina would move back into the hotel today and stay there for the duration of the training session.

She refilled her cup, walked to the round oak breakfast table and took a seat.

Jake straddled one of the wooden chairs across the table from her. "Are you always an early riser or do you have a lot of last-minute preparations left to take care of?"

"Not too many, but I'll touch base with my guest instructors to make certain they know exactly what to expect and what we need from them."

Small talk, surely not why he'd wanted a conversation.

He sipped his coffee. "What kind of guest instructors do you need for a riding camp? Seems a couple of good wranglers could handle that."

"Actually, my lead volunteers are all excellent horsewomen, and all the ranches we're using have knowledgeable wranglers. It's handling troubled girls, most between thirteen and fourteen, that baffles them."

"That, I can identify with."

The tension began to ease. As long as they kept things simple and businesslike between them, she'd be able to pull this off. It was only when she let thoughts of R.J. take over that the resentment began to simmer. Or when one of those bizarre sensual reactions hit.

"Sounds like you could use an office to work from today," Jake said. "You are welcome to use mine, and if you need any printers, copiers, et cetera, they're available at ranch headquarters."

"I appreciate the offer, but the hotel has a well-equipped business office for guests."

"You never know how many people might be using that."

"True, but I'm sure I can schedule around them." She was starting to see where this was going, but it was hard to believe he actually wanted her here as a houseguest.

"If you're still worried about issues with Thad, you can relax," she said. "Mildred talked to Sheriff Garcia last night. She just has to pick up the restraining order forms, fill them out and fax them to Garcia."

"Actually, we can file them here in Austin. Garcia assured me he'd follow up to see that the process is expedited and that Thad is served the papers ASAP."

"When did you talk to Garcia?"

"Last night. He called after he talked to you and Mildred."

Her emotions flared. "Garcia had no right to involve you in this any more than you already are. I definitely didn't ask him to."

"He's concerned about you and Mildred. Frankly, so am I. Caffey's dangerous and unpredictable. You can't take chances with a psycho like that."

"He's a monster, but he's not stupid. As soon as he realizes that harassing Mildred will lead to his arrest, he'll back off. He's surely had enough of life behind bars."

"Makes sense, but risky to second-guess a man like Caffey."

Carolina took a sip of coffee, adding caffeine to her rattled nerves. This was growing more complicated by the second.

If they didn't get this training session in this week, they'd be forced to cancel next month's camps in the Austin area. So many needy children would be disappointed, so many opportunities to make a difference in their lives lost.

"If you want to back out of our arrangement, I'll understand. I know this is more than you bargained for."

"And then what would you do at this late date?"

"I could possibly move it to the Bent Pine."

"I thought the whole purpose of having it in the Austin area was so the volunteers didn't have to travel and be away from their own homes for five nights."

"It was, but—"

He put up a hand to halt her words. "No backing out, not after offering to save my daughter from herself for a few weeks this summer. Besides, Sheriff Garcia and I both agree that there's no reason to let Thad Caffey interfere with your plans. We just need a few rules of engagement."

"Such as?"

"From now until the session is over or Thad is behind bars, whichever comes first, you and Mildred won't leave the ranch without me or one of my wranglers with you. On the off chance Thad is foolish enough to show up here, I or the wranglers will be sure that he's entertained appropriately until the law arrives to arrest him."

She shook her head. "I appreciate the offer, but I can't ask you to give up your privacy."

A seductive smile touched the corners of his mouth. "I have a huge house on over two thousand acres of land. I think I can find a bit of privacy if or when I need it."

It was still asking a lot, especially considering their prior relationship. "You don't have to do this."

"Sure I do. What kind of selfish rat would I be to deny kids a month on a ranch? Besides, I'm intrigued with the whole Saddle-Up project. In spite of what you think, I'm not totally heartless."

The perfect segue into his treatment of R.J., but he was saying all the right things, doing the right things. And she needed his ranch. Jumping him at this point would be ludicrous.

"My staying here would be awkward," she said honestly.

"It's six days, Carolina. Not a marriage proposal and we're adults."

"In that case, I accept your offer—until Thad is arrested. But first I have to go back to the hotel, pick up our luggage and check out. Then I need to run a couple of errands in town."

"No problem. While we're out, Mildred can stop off at Judge DeWitt's office, fill out and file the needed papers to get the order of protection started."

"Who is Judge DeWitt?"

"A friend of mine. Garcia is going to call him this morning and fill him in on the situation."

Another decision she'd been left out of. But, after all, this was Mildred's dilemma, not hers, to micromanage. "I'm sure Mildred will appreciate that."

Jake finished his coffee, carried his mug to the sink and rinsed it.

"Edna will be here about six to cook breakfast and talk your head off. If you want something before that, help yourself to whatever you see that you want. Give me an hour or so heads-up before you're ready to go into Austin. I have to take care of a few things on the ranch first. Edna has my cell phone number."

"It really isn't necessary that anyone go with us to the hotel. Security is excellent there and you have a ranch to run."

"The rules of engagement, remember? And the cows won't miss me."

She watched as he walked away, hating that he seemed so cool with all this when she knew he didn't want her here. Hating that Garcia had enlisted him as their protector.

Hating most of all that she was starting to like the man.

Six more days. Avoiding him was no longer an option. He'd made the decision to force them to engage.

So before she left the Silver Spur on Sunday afternoon, the issue of his treatment toward R.J. would come to a head. The elephant in the room could not be ignored forever.

CAROLINA CLIMBED INTO the backseat as they left Judge DeWitt's office, leaving Mildred to sit in the front with Jake. She had to admit that Jake was good for Mildred, managed to pull her into conversations that didn't center on Thad. He'd even coaxed laughter from her a few times.

In the bright light of day with life in full swing all around her, Thad Caffey felt more like a bump in the asphalt to Carolina than the roadblock he'd seemed last night. There was a good chance they'd all overreacted, a fact that would no doubt please Thad.

"Filing the restraining order was liberating," Mildred said as they pulled back into traffic. "Not that I want Thad to go back to prison. I know it sounds crazy, but I hope he has changed and that he is able to go on with his life as a decent citizen—just not with me."

"Doesn't sound crazy to me," Jake said. "You loved him enough to marry him. He must have had some good qualities."

"I was convinced of it at the time. However, I was seventeen, living on my own after years in foster care, and had never had anyone tell me they loved me."

"Where were your parents?"

"There was never a dad. I mean, there had to be one, but his name wasn't on the birth certificate. Mother was addicted to heroin and crack cocaine. She overdosed when I was six."

"That had to be rough."

"The saddest thing of all is I barely remember her. Foster care was never terrible. My marriage to Thad is the incomparable nightmare chapter of my life."

The nightmare chapter of life.

Unbidden, the words triggered memories that never failed to drag Carolina back to her own darkest days. One phone call from an unfamiliar voice and her world had plunged into darkness.

The private jet carrying Hugh and his friends home from a Dallas Cowboys game had crashed in an isolated area of West Texas. There were no survivors.

She'd forced herself to go on, calling on all the energy she possessed to plow through each day.

And then God dropped a miracle into her life. Her son Damien found a frightened and injured woman named Emma and baby Belle wandering across their ranch in a rare Dallas area snowstorm. Damien had become Emma's hero.

Baby Belle had become Carolina's. Having a baby in the house to love and cuddle had revived her as nothing else could have.

Life had changed a lot since then. Now all three of her sons were happily married and the big house overflowed with love and children. She'd never stopped missing Hugh, but she'd moved on, just as Mildred was doing, though their situations weren't the least bit similar.

The most poignant difference was that Carolina had known true love, the kind no one should ever expect to find more than once in a lifetime.

Fifteen minutes later, Jake pulled up in front of the hotel. He stepped out of the truck and scanned the area, no doubt making certain Thad had not made good on his threat to be waiting for their return.

Carolina half expected to see Thad step out of the midday shadows, but fortunately there was no sign of him.

In minutes they were walking through the hotel and taking the elevator to the two-bedroom suite.

"All clear," Jake said, as they approached the door.

"Don't count on that," Mildred said. "It would be like Thad to be inside, stretched out on the bed watching TV, waiting, just as he said."

Mildred's voice trembled, a reminder to Carolina of how much she feared her ex.

Carolina linked her arm with Mildred's. "The hotel would never give him a key."

"I'll stick my head in first and make sure there are no surprises," Jake assured them. Carolina handed him the key.

Jake entered, walked across the spacious living area and opened the drapes, letting in a golden sweep of sunshine and revealing the breathtaking city view. Once he'd taken a peek into the bedrooms and bathrooms, he came back to the door and ushered them inside.

"Nice digs. No wonder you weren't excited about leaving this place."

"All the comforts of home," she said—a huge exaggeration. As luxurious as the suite was, she was never as at home as she was on the Bent Pine Ranch. But she would have been far more at home here than she was going to be sleeping in Jake's guest room and risking running into him every time she ventured out.

She did a visual sweep of the area. Everything looked exactly as they'd left it. For all they knew, Thad might not even have been in Austin when he sent the text, much less waiting for them at the hotel.

Wife beaters tended to also play fast and loose with the truth. That was just one of the many facts she'd learned about spousal abuse since befriending Mildred.

"It won't take me but a few minutes to pack," Mildred said. "I'd like to get out of here as quickly as possible, just in case Thad is outside and was watching when we arrived." She went into her bedroom and closed the door behind her.

Jake followed Carolina into the other bedroom. "Do you need some help with packing, perhaps take care of the hanging clothes?"

"No. I can handle it."

"Now, why does that not surprise me?"

"You make independence sound like a bad thing."

"It can be, if it's taken too far."

"We're not still talking about packing, are we?" Carolina asked.

"Not necessarily."

"The truth is I'm only taking a few things with me," she said. "Garcia's rules of engagement are only in effect until Thad is arrested or no longer a threat. I expect that to be long before I drive back to Oak Grove on Sunday afternoon."

"Is accepting my hospitality that unpleasant for you?"

She took a deep breath and exhaled slowly. "Can you honestly say you want me at the Silver Spur after the accusation you hurled at me on the phone a week ago?"

Jake stepped closer, in her space, his stare piercing. "We're getting nowhere talking around this. We're both adults. Hit me with your best shot and then hopefully we can move past R.J. and deal with the situation at hand."

Her best shot. Why not? She might not get this chance again. Still, she should play this smart.

But once the words started coming, her emotions took over and all her frustration spilled out.

"What kind of coldhearted, merciless, intolerant, unforgiving man would deprive his dying father of even hearing his voice on the phone?"

Chapter Nine

Jake winced at the bombardment of adjectives. "Don't mince words on my account."

"You said to hit you with my best shot."

"I wasn't expecting it would be from a shotgun."

"I may have gotten a bit carried away," Carolina admitted, "but I'm being honest. I understand why you don't have a lot of love or respect for R.J. He was a failure as a father and a rotten husband. He admits that."

"He couldn't very well deny it."

"No, but people can change."

"By screwing up his adult children's lives—as if he didn't do enough of that while we were kids?"

"He's not screwing up their lives. He's reached out and reunited with every one of his six children but you. They've become a loving and close-knit family. If you weren't too contrary to visit them at the Dry Gulch, you'd see that for yourself."

"I have no desire to be part of R.J.'s attempt at guilt resolution."

"What about Lizzie? Doesn't she deserve the chance to get to know her grandfather?"

"So she can be part of the trap?"

"What trap?" Carolina demanded.

"That bizarre will he concocted."

"I admit the original will was a bit unorthodox, but it's not as bizarre as it seems and certainly not a trap."

Not surprising that she'd back the will, since she'd likely been in on the idea from the beginning. "What do you call it when all you have to do to be included in his will is give up your lifestyle and career and move onto the Dry Gulch Ranch to pay homage to a man who never gave two cents about you when you needed him?"

"A second chance."

"A second chance for R.J. For everyone else it's a train wreck, or it will be when the money runs out and the infighting starts. The Dry Gulch can't possibly support that many families over the long haul. Imagine the bitter resentment when it blows up in their face. Of course R.J. will be long gone by then."

"Think what you want to. You will anyway." Carolina walked over to the closet and began removing clothes from their hangers and placing them on the bed.

The conversation had solved nothing. This whole R.J. thing had become a crusade with her.

She tossed several shirts to the bed. "You have everything wrong. In the beginning, the will might have been overly demanding, but none of that matters now. All the manipulative demands of the will have been eliminated one by one."

"Were the changes your idea, too?"

Her hands flew to her hips. "What did you say?"

"R.J. admitted from the beginning that you were behind the will. I just wondered if you authorized the changes, as well."

She stared at him as if he were speaking Greek. "So that's why you accused me of screwing over the Daltons? You think I talked R.J. into all that. For the record, R.J. came to me when he was diagnosed with an inoperable brain tumor and said he wanted to leave the Dry Gulch to me to keep it out of the hands of developers. I suggested he leave it to his family. The will itself was all R.J.'s doing."

R.J. had wanted to give her the land and she'd refused. That bit of new information blew the hell out of his theory that she was looking to step up and buy the ranch when the family-ties fiasco fell apart.

Carolina stopped for a quick breath and then seemed to gain steam in her verbal assault. Nothing he didn't deserve.

"You should get your facts straight before you make snap judgments about people or situations, Jake Dalton. The Dry Gulch doesn't have to financially support all the Daltons. Leif is a defense attorney. Travis is a Dallas homicide detective. Cannon is raising rodeo bulls and broncs. Jade lives with her navy SEAL husband, who's stationed in San Diego. Adam is the one who actually manages the ranch and does a great job at it."

"I stand corrected." And feeling extremely guilty.

Not for misjudging R.J. Jake's reasons for resenting his biological father ran a lot deeper than the manipulative will. Reasons he would not indulge to Carolina today or any other day.

But he had been a real jerk where Carolina was concerned.

He met her steely gaze. "I've been way out of line. I jumped to conclusions and made a fool of myself. I'm sorry for crediting any of that will to you."

She looked at him, the anger subsiding as a look of pleading burned in her eyes. "I don't care what you think of me, Jake, but I'm begging you to contact your father, soon, before it's too late. It would mean the world to him—and to me."

Jake's insides clenched. It was tearing him apart to look into her eyes and refuse her, but she had no idea what she was asking of him.

"I'll think about it." That was the most he could promise.

"Then I guess I'll have to settle with that for now." She turned away and resumed packing, leaving more behind than she was taking.

A protective urge hit hard and fast. Caffey hadn't been waiting today. That didn't make him any less a threat in Jake's mind. "I know I don't really have a say in the matter, but I'd really like it if you'd just take everything and spend the rest of the week at the Silver Spur."

"Why?"

To keep her safe. To keep her close. He wasn't sure exactly which need was stronger at this moment. "Because if you leave the Silver Spur, I'll be forced to move into the hotel to watch your back, and I truly hate city life and hotels."

"For once we agree on something."

NINETY MINUTES AND a full stomach later, Carolina was still second-guessing her decision to check out of the hotel. If Caffey was arrested, there would be no logical reason for her to infringe on Jake's hospitality.

When she lost her cool and unloaded her frustration and anger on him back at the hotel, she'd half expected him to immediately renege on his offer of the Silver Spur Ranch. Instead his protective edge had taken over.

He'd even apologized for assuming she'd had something to do with R.J.'s will. She didn't fully understand why he was so angered by the will, though the terms had pretty much excluded him.

He had the Silver Spur to run. There was no way he'd have left his ranch to help manage the Dry Gulch. Then again he didn't need the money or the land, so why let the will keep him from doing the right thing by R.J.?

His resentment had to be triggered by something more. At least a promise to think about connecting with R.J. had come out of the confrontation. That was an improvement over where they were before the heated discussion this morning.

At any rate, Jake didn't appear to be harboring a grudge against her. If anything, he seemed more relaxed since they'd brought everything into the open. And it definitely hadn't had a negative effect on his appetite.

The first stop after leaving the hotel had been

a neighborhood Italian trattoria with checkered tablecloths, mismatched chairs and mouthwatering odors. Mama Giada, the plump matron of the Italian family, had greeted Jake with laughter and a warm hug. He was obviously a much-liked regular in the restaurant.

They weren't offered a menu. Instead Mama Giada and her staff served them family-style, the round table laden with overflowing platters of antipasto, lasagna, and spaghetti and meatballs—all apparently Jake's favorites. And then Mama Giada had insisted they stay for dessert—huge servings of creamy tiramisu and steaming cups of cappuccino.

Jake was the only one who'd done the food justice. Like her sons, he had that ravenous rancher's appetite. Not that you'd guess that by looking at Jake's hard, lean body and six-pack abs.

"That will keep me fueled for a few hours," Jake said as they left the restaurant. "What's on the agenda for the rest of the afternoon?"

"For starters, we need to stop somewhere and stock up on bottled water, soft drinks, instant tea and lots of ice. Beverages will be in high demand in this heat and humidity."

"Snacks and fruit, too," Mildred added.

"Before we buy all that, we need to give Edna a call. I suspect she's had the oven full of cookies all day and probably already called Gus's market and ordered bottled drinks and lots of extra ice."

"Surely not," Carolina lamented. "I already feel terrible that she's having to deal with un-expected houseguests."

"I told her you could handle it, but I can't guarantee she listened. In case you haven't picked up on it already, Edna works for me in name only. In actuality, she runs the house and orders everyone around—except Mother. Mother is the queen, thankfully a benevolent one who adores her granddaughter and toler-ates me."

His mother, Mary, R.J.'s first wife, though she was the one wife Carolina had never heard R.J. mention. Not that he ever talked much about any of his ex-wives. The only woman whose memory still seemed to haunt him was someone he called Gwen.

They weren't even sure Gwen was real, since R.J. asked for her or talked to her only when he fell into one of his confused states.

But it would be interesting to meet R.J.'s first wife. Getting to know her might explain Jake's treatment of R.J. The queen might even be the tipping mechanism that could change Jake's mind about contacting R.J.

"I can't wait to get to meet your mother," Carolina said.

"You'll get your chance tomorrow."

"I thought she wasn't coming home until the weekend."

"Change of plans. New York is also hot and muggy, so they decided they might as well head back to Texas—after they see *The Phantom of the Opera* tonight."

"Good for them. She'll love it."

"She knows. This will make about her tenth time to see it."

"Sounds like a woman who knows what she likes. But a ranch full of women and two unexpected houseguests. That might upset a Texas queen."

"Not this queen. She rolls with the punches, occasionally delivering a few of her own."

"Then I'll definitely stay out of her way."

Jake pulled into traffic before he made the call on the car's speaker system. As soon as he made the connection, Edna burst into her own agenda.

"I've made blackberry cobbler for dinner tonight. I hope you two ladies like cobbler. I picked the berries myself."

"Love it," Mildred said.

"I love all kinds of cobblers, but blackberry

is my favorite," Carolina said truthfully. "But I hope you didn't go to all that trouble for us."

"Wasn't a bit of trouble. Made so many cobblers in my life I could do it in my sleep and still have the crust come out a golden brown."

"And delicious, I'm sure."

"Don't get many complaints around the Silver Spur," Edna admitted.

"Is that all you baked?" Jake asked.

"No use to heat up the oven for just one cobbler. I baked a few dozen chocolate chip cookies and some blueberry muffins. I figured the volunteers will need some nibbles. That store-bought stuff is hardly fit to eat."

"I'm sure we'll love anything you make, but you're going to spoil us and wear yourself out. Keep this up and Jake won't ever let us come back to the ranch after the training session is over."

Not that she ever expected to.

"I'm through with the baking for today, and I'm not a bit tuckered out," Edna continued. "Oh, and before I forget, I ordered a few cases of bottled water and soft drinks from Gus's market. He's gonna have his grandson deliver them in the morning, already iced down and ready to quench the thirst."

"You keep this up and Carolina's going to

fire me as the training leader and hire you," Mildred said.

"Not a chance. But I like helping when I can. Doing for others is good for the soul."

"I agree," Carolina said. "But now you've done more than enough."

"What will you do about lunches for the volunteers?" Edna asked.

"The food is all ordered from a caterer in Austin—simple lunches that we can eat picnic-style on the ranch. One of the volunteers will be picking that up on her way here every morning. Really, the food situation is under control."

"I didn't mean to go steppin' on your toes," Edna said. "If I do, you just tell me. I can call Gus back and cancel that order if you want me to."

"Absolutely not. You just saved us an hour of shopping. I can't thank you enough, but please don't do more. I hate putting you out like this."

"Don't you go fretting a minute about that, Mrs. Lambert. I'm tickled pink to be busy. Nothing I like better than cooking for a full table of hungry folks."

And after the lunch they'd just eaten, Carolina might not be hungry again until this time tomorrow.

They finished the conversation, and Carolina

went back to her to-do list. "I think we can by-pass grocery shopping."

"So, where do we go from here?" Jake asked.

"Sheplers, to pick up one hundred and fifty white straw Western hats."

"Now you're talking," Jake said. "Can't be a cowgirl without the appropriate hat and boots."

"Unfortunately, the budget didn't stretch to boots," Mildred said. "But we did get jeans, shorts, T-shirts, undies and socks, and one authentic Western shirt for each girl in the program."

"I'm impressed."

"It's as much necessary as generous," Carolina admitted. "Many of the girls don't have appropriate clothing. Having them all dress similarly avoids hurt feelings and worries about fitting in. And it keeps the counselors from having to outlaw some of the more revealing shorts and tops the girls show up in."

"Like the ones my daughter wears," Jake said.

"Sometimes far worse, believe me," Carolina said.

"Hard to imagine." Jake took the freeway ramp. "Still seems like the girls need cowboy boots, especially if they try kicking a cow chip on a hot day."

"That's a gross thought. Actually, we usually do have to buy a few pairs of shoes for the girls who show up with nothing but flip-flops."

"And everything is bought with donations?"

"Yes, and most of that donated by Carolina," Mildred said. "And that's only a smidgen of all the contributions the Lamberts make to worthy causes around the state and the globe."

"So I've heard." He flicked on the lane change signal. "Is it too late for another donation, one that would cover the cost of a hundred and fifty pairs of cowboy boots?"

"It's never too late to accept boots if you're buying."

"I'm buying. Never count a coldhearted, ruthless man out."

Now he was mocking her, but she could handle that. "I'm not sure we can find that many boots in the right sizes on such short notice."

"Are you kidding? It's Texas. And I can be very persuasive when I need to be."

"I've noticed."

"How will you fit all the girls?" Mildred asked. "Western hats only come in a few sizes and we get a variety that usually works. But shoes have to be a good fit."

"If I'm buying one hundred and fifty pairs of boots, the company can send someone out to fit them."

"All the girls attend orientation at Sara and

Jess's ranch a week from next Monday," Carolina said. "That would be a good time to fit them into the boots. After that, they'll be scattered to ten different ranches for the duration of the month."

"We'll work it out one way or another," Jake said. "I don't want it said I let cowgirls go without boots."

He was doing it again, screwing with all Carolina's preconceptions about him. He was both protective and generous, a caring father and close to his mother—all traits she admired.

It must have been something more than a will that turned him against his father. Whatever it was, it was time to let it go—for his sake and R.J.'s.

True to his word, once they arrived at the Western shop, Jake made all the arrangements to purchase the boots, though some would have to be shipped directly from the supplier to Sara's ranch. Salesmen would show up the day of the fitting to make sure every girl got boots.

Apparently Jake had a great deal of clout with the shop and no shortage of attention from the female clerks. Widowed, wealthy, gorgeous and not totally heartless—it was amazing he'd managed to stay single for so long.

Carolina perused the shop while Jake helped load the boxes of hats into his pickup truck.

When he rejoined them inside, his cell phone was stuck to his ear and he did not look happy.

Dread knotted in her stomach. Her first impression was that this must be Thad again.

Chapter Ten

As soon as Jake had broken the connection with Sheriff Garcia, Carolina was at his elbow asking if anything was wrong. He wouldn't lie to her, but he managed to put her off until they were in the truck and headed back to the ranch. Unfortunately that reprieve only lasted until he'd started the engine and backed out of his parking space.

"So, what is it you didn't want to talk about in the shop?"

"The call was from Garcia. Nothing terrible, so don't go jumping to conclusions."

Carolina groaned. "What is Thad up to now?"

"No one's exactly sure. That's the problem."

"Has he been served with the restraining order?" Mildred asked.

"Not yet. Have to find him first."

"I gave them his address."

"He wasn't there. They ran into a problem locating him."

"Then he must still be in Austin," Carolina said, "still hoping to lure Mildred into meeting him."

"At this point he could be anywhere," Jake said. "What made you think he was living at his hunting camp?"

"I just assumed it," Mildred admitted. "It's the only property he owns. It's where he went when he claimed he needed alone time, so it would have been natural for him to go there long enough to get his act together."

"According to Garcia, it doesn't appear that he is living in the camp now or that anyone else has stayed there in a very long time."

Carolina leaned forward, a hand on the back of Jake's seat. "How did he reach that conclusion?"

"No clothes in the closet or the drawers. No food in the house. No electricity. Spider webs across the doors. Several scorpions crawling along the uneven floorboards."

"Spiders and scorpions. Throw in some rats and Jake should have felt right at home," Carolina said.

"How did they get in the cabin if Thad wasn't there?" Mildred asked.

"They didn't have to break in. Half of the

windows were broken or missing and the back door was ajar. Basically it's a deserted camp house. Do you know of a friend Caffey might be staying with?"

"No. He didn't really have friends. He got along with people at the feed store where he worked the stockroom, but he didn't see them after work. He was always a loner. The defense couldn't find even one person to attest under oath to his good character."

"Well, he has to live somewhere unless he's sleeping in his car," Jake said. "Or does he even have a car?"

"He was driving the same old truck he had before he was convicted when we were accosted by him at the parking lot. I'm guessing someone kept that for him while he was in prison."

"So they found nothing at the camp to indicate Thad had been there?" Carolina said, more statement than question.

"It's doubtful he's been living inside the camp, but it is possible that he's been living in his truck on the property—maybe even likely."

"Why do you think that?" Carolina asked.

"Garcia and his deputy found dozens of empty beer cans and cigarette butts near the camp house. It was clear they hadn't been there long. There were also empty shell casings scattered around the dirt area behind the house as if someone had used the area within the last few days for target practice."

"How would Jake get a gun?" Carolina broke in. "He's committed a felony. I'm certain no one around Oak Grove would have sold it to him, and the authorities definitely didn't let him keep his hunting guns after he was found guilty."

"An Oak Grove resident had his house broken into four days ago. Nothing was taken but some cash, an electronic tablet and two guns—a rifle and an automatic pistol. That syncs with the recently fired shells they found on the property, though there's no forensics available on that."

"Burglary and the illegal possession of guns," Carolina said. "That's enough to arrest Thad right now without waiting for him to break the rules of a restraining order."

"*Suspected* burglary and possession of firearms," Jake reminded her. "That's only a theory at this point. There's no concrete evidence as yet to back that up."

"And that doesn't change the fact that they can't arrest him if they can't find him." Angst reduced Mildred's words to a shaky whisper. "It's not hunting season. If Thad stole guns, he plans to use them either to force me to get back together with him or to pay me back for the testimony that sent him to prison."

Jake had to agree with her logic. But why

steal guns to shoot Mildred when he'd always resorted to using his fists against her before?

"That settles it," Mildred said. "My continuing problems with Thad will be a distraction for the Silver Spur and the training program. It's time for me to go home."

"You can't just go home without a bodyguard at this point," Carolina said. "Maybe we should cancel the training program."

Jake's chest tightened, his muscles bunching beneath his shirt. Carolina belonged to one of the wealthiest families in Texas. All the protection money could buy was hers for the asking. He should be glad for her to take all these problems off his hands.

But he could hear the anxiety in her voice. She clearly hated disappointing those kids, but she was torn between that and putting anyone in danger.

Only he had worries of his own where her safety was concerned.

"If protection is the only issue, I can't imagine you'll find any place safer than the Silver Spur," Jake said. "Caffey is a stinking coward who beats up women. He's not going to come charging onto the ranch with as many wranglers as we have to take him on. If he does, we have him."

"Having your wranglers doing duty as bodyguards hardly seems fair to you," Carolina said. "What will your mother think of this?"

"You can ask her yourself tomorrow, but I guarantee she'll tell you not to dare let a man like Thad Caffey shut down your program."

"It's not that I'm afraid," Carolina argued. "I was giving you an out."

"I'm not looking for one."

"Are you sure?"

"Wouldn't say so if I didn't mean it."

"In that case, there really is no reason for Mildred to leave or for us to cancel."

Relief relaxed Jake's strained muscles. He had no doubt that he could keep both Mildred and Carolina safe—as long as they were here on the Silver Spur.

But he couldn't make them stay forever. Five more days and Carolina would be gone.

Off his ranch. Out of his life. Exactly what he'd wanted yesterday morning.

So why was the prospect of her leaving sounding so damned upsetting now?

LIZZIE TURNED UP her radio and began twirling around the room to the beat of the latest Taylor Swift tune. The summer she'd already given up on as being a monotonous drag was looking up.

Carolina Lambert had surprised her at dinner tonight by actually inviting her to work not only

with the women this week but as a junior counselor for the whole month of July. Even more
surprising, her father had agreed to let her do it.

It might not be the most exciting summer she
could have had, but it beat hanging around here
all day. Her three best friends were either trav-
eling or working. And her dad would ground
her forever if he found out she'd sneaked out
to see Calvin.

Her phone rang. Calvin—again. She started
to ignore it, but if she did, he'd only keep calling until she answered.

"Hello," she said, already wary, knowing
what he wanted.

"Hi, baby. Where are you?"

"In my room."

"By yourself?"

"Yeah. Just hanging out and watching MTV."

"You'd be having more fun hanging out with
me."

"Until Dad killed me."

"Tell him you're going to Angie's."

"I can't keep lying to him."

"You won't have to. I might be gone from
this boring town soon. That's why I gotta see
you, baby."

"Are you in trouble again?"

"Same old stuff. The sheriff still thinks I had

something to do with breaking into Bilson's Liquor Store last weekend."

"Did you?"

"No. I told you that already. But Mom is on the warpath and threatening to send me to live with my dad and his new wife up in Oklahoma."

"For the summer?"

"For good." He spit out a stream of foul language that made her cringe. "Don't worry, baby. I've got a plan. I'm not staying with that tyrant and his bitch. And I'm not going anywhere without you."

The comment made her uneasy. She definitely wasn't running off with him. "What kind of plan?"

"Meet me tonight and I'll tell you all about it."

"I can't. We have houseguests. My dad expects me to help entertain them," she lied.

She hated lying to anyone, especially Calvin or her dad, but she seemed to be doing it more and more lately. She'd love to tell Calvin her news, but it would seem kind of heartless with his life in such a mess.

"Are you coming to meet me?" he urged.

"I said I can't."

"So you're just going to let your dad run your life?" he challenged.

She let the question go unanswered. At sixteen she didn't have a lot of choice. If Calvin had listened to his mother she wouldn't be sending him away. Pointing that out would only make him mad at her.

"I'll be waiting for you at our secret spot just north of your gate," he said. "Make it happen. You know you want to, Lizzie." He broke the connection without bothering to say goodbye.

Typical Calvin. Everything was about him. He'd be furious if she didn't show. Dating the school bad boy had been exciting at first, but when things didn't go his way, he could be downright scary.

She felt shaky inside as she tossed the phone to the bed. She walked over to her dresser, picked up her lip gloss and took a good look at herself in the mirror.

It was a wonder Calvin had ever asked her out in the first place when he could have dated almost any girl in the school. She wasn't beautiful, not the way her mother had been.

Lizzie's long reddish-brown hair curled at the ends, whereas her mother's had hung straight to her narrow shoulders. Lizzie's nose was sprinkled with freckles and there was always a pimple waiting to pop up on her face.

Her mother's skin had been flawless. The picture of the two of them Lizzie kept on top of her chest was a constant reminder of her mother's beauty. It was the other memories that were slowly slipping away. The memories that had held her together in the horrifying days and months after her death.

Poignant images of her mother holding tight to her hand the first day of kindergarten. Echoes of her mother's laughter as they baked cookies on cool Saturday afternoons or rode their bikes to the park. Warm, fuzzy memories of her mother sliding into bed beside her and cuddling when she'd wake up screaming from a nightmare.

Sleep well and sweet dreams, princess. Love you.

Those were the last words Lizzie would hear before her mother turned off the light each night.

They were the last words she ever heard her mother utter.

An old familiar ache settled inside her, not so much for the mother she could barely remember, but for the mother who wasn't here now.

The lip gloss fell from her fingers and rolled onto the floor. Not everything was about Calvin. Lizzie had needs, too. If her mother were here, she'd understand.

The mother who only existed in a picture frame on Lizzie's dresser.

BY ALL RIGHTS, Jake should be miserable this morning. He wasn't. In fact he was feeling a lot like his old self—confident, energetic and ready to tackle the world, including Thad Caffey.

There was no easy explanation for it, at least not one he was ready to examine closely. But Lizzie definitely had something to do with it.

She'd shown up for breakfast this morning in a good mood and actually engaged in table conversation. Well, primarily she'd talked to Carolina, but still, she'd been pleasant and involved. He didn't understand the rapidly developing bond between them, but he wasn't knocking it.

Right after breakfast, Jake had called a conference with all the wranglers. They'd met at headquarters for coffee and some of Edna's homemade muffins. She'd made enough he could have shared with the entire neighborhood and still have more than enough left for Carolina's gang.

He'd presented the basics, and his workers had reacted as expected—exuberant and loud. Dealing with a wife beater on their turf was obviously a lot more exciting than the routine ranch work they were used to.

Jake couldn't locate any pictures of Caffey on the internet that resembled the man they'd run into at the capitol, so he was forced to rely on an oral description. Not perfect, but close enough they'd recognize him if they caught him sneaking around the spread. Not that they wouldn't have checked out any man who showed up where he had no business.

Jake had full control of gate security today. The automatic monitor would send the entrance request directly to his cell phone. If the system was tampered with in any way, he'd also get a signal. The gate wouldn't open without his knowing it.

The strings of barbwire fences were another story. They did a great job of keeping in the cows, but needless to say the wire could be cut or crashed through without too much trouble.

Not a problem in this situation. If the yellow-bellied coward was crazy enough to trespass, he'd never get anywhere near the Saddle-Up team or the house before he was noticed and apprehended.

Protection was taken care of. Unfortunately, Jake's unexpected attraction to Carolina was giving him more problems than ever. When they accidentally brushed shoulders in the kitchen that morning, he'd felt another hit to his libido. He couldn't just avoid her, so he had to find some way to put this in perspective.

Jake was almost back to the horse barn now.

He'd get one of the wranglers to take care of Riley and then put the stallion out to pasture until afternoon.

He tugged on the reins and circled around a cluster of scrawny mesquite trees until he had a good view of Carolina's meeting spot. He had offered the air-conditioned conference room at headquarters for their kickoff that morning, but Carolina had decided that a pine-strewn, shady spot near the horse barns would be more in keeping with the atmosphere of the camps they'd be conducting in the heat of summer.

She was definitely not the wealthy, pampered socialite he'd thought her before he got to know her.

The thirty women had brought and set up their own chairs like soccer moms ready for a big game. Carolina was standing in front of the group behind a metal folding table Tilson had brought down from headquarters.

Jake's cell phone rang—the automated gate security system letting him know someone was requesting entrance. He changed it to the security-camera view and the image of a middle-aged guy with a receding hairline, a sprinkling of dusky-colored facial hair and a pair of wire-rimmed glasses.

Definitely not Caffey.

"Good morning. Welcome to the Silver Spur. How can I help you?"

"I'm Dr. James Otis. I'm supposed to meet Carolina Lambert here this morning. Actually I'm running a bit late. Drove right by the turn-off to this place and had to double back. I do believe this is officially rural living."

"Yep. Home, home on the range, a half mile from the end of nowhere."

Jake recognized the name from the list Carolina had provided him. Otis was an Austin psychiatrist who specialized in helping parents cope with unruly teens. His teen boot camps had gained national attention.

"When the gate opens, just follow the main blacktop road back to the big house. I'll meet you there and walk you out to where Carolina's group is meeting. It's only a short walk."

"I'd appreciate that, unless it's the walk that leads anywhere near those giant Texas long-horns I saw on the way here. Oh, and no snakes, either, especially the ones who carry their own rattle. I find them to be extremely antisocial."

"You drive a hard bargain, but I'll try to accommodate you."

And then he'd go back to dealing with his livestock. He didn't need a shrink messing with his mind. He had a good mood going. No reason to risk losing that.

CAROLINA WELCOMED DR. OTIS and then turned him over to Mildred for introduction to the group. When she stood back and looked around, Jake was already walking away.

She ran to catch up with him.

"If you have some time, you should stay and listen to the doctor's talk. You might get some insight into the communication problems you're having with Lizzie."

"Communication problems? Is that what you call it when your daughter rolls her eyes at everything you say?"

"I've never had a daughter, so I won't begin to pretend I know what you're dealing with. But I've heard Dr. Otis speak before. I think you'd get something out of his talk."

Jake looked back toward the group. "One man in a group of women. I'd feel like the lone rooster at a hen party."

"You're not worried about damaging your manhood, are you?" she teased.

"Nope. Worried about the teasing from a group of macho cowboys. Tell you what, why don't you listen and then we'll go horseback riding when you finish up with your meetings today and you can share what you think I need to hear?"

"It doesn't work that way."

"It could. But don't worry about it. I know

you're busy. I'll get out of here and let you get back to work."

She should let it go at that, but the truth was she wanted to go riding with Jake. She couldn't come up with a reason for it, but she knew she wanted to spend time with him. Away from Mildred. Away from constant talk of Thad Caffey, which had basically been the center of almost every conversation up until now.

"I'd like to go riding with you, but we don't finish until after four. What time are you expecting your mother?"

"Not before six thirty, but that's okay. It was just a thought."

"Are you reneging on your invitation?"

"No," he said. "Just giving you an easy way out."

"In that case I'll meet you at the horse barn a few minutes after four."

He tipped his hat and smiled. "See you then."

Her pulse raced. It must be from too much sun.

CAROLINA CHOSE A packaged chicken and an avocado/spinach/goat cheese wrap from one of the caterer's baskets and a soft drink from a large cooler. A few of the women took their food back to their chairs. Most wandered over to one of the wooden picnic tables a few of the wranglers had set up while they were role-playing problem situations with Dr. Otis. Carolina had no idea where they'd obtained the tables on such short notice.

Carolina took her sandwich and walked to a huge tree stump near the fenced corral where a half dozen magnificent horses were grazing contentedly. All in all it had been a successful but busy morning, leaving her little time to fret about Thad Caffey or contemplate her promised afternoon ride with Jake.

He'd certainly been quick enough to back off when he thought she wasn't interested. Only she'd wanted to accept and her motivation hadn't just been her love for riding. She liked him. There was no denying it any more than she could deny that he got to her on some inexplicable sensual level.

It was the first time she'd experienced anything like that since Hugh's death.

She wasn't ready for that. She might never be, but definitely not yet. Nor had Jake given any indication that he was interested in her as a woman.

"Mind if I join you?"

Carolina looked up at Lizzie's voice. She'd been so lost in her own thoughts she hadn't realized Lizzie was there.

"Of course I don't mind. I'd love to hear what

you thought of Dr. Otis and the morning's activities. Unfortunately you can't just pull up a stump, but we can move to a table."

"I'd rather stay here where it's private. I don't mind standing, since the grass is too wet to sit on."

"Then by all means, let's chat. What is it you want to talk about?"

"Dr. Otis. He's really smart. I don't know how he knows so much about teenage girls, but I could relate to a lot of what he said."

"Good. Anything in particular?"

"That stuff about boyfriends, how you get all these mixed emotions when you're with them."

"The war between your hormones and your judgment?"

"Yeah. I guess that's it. At first guys like you the way you are, but then they want to own you."

"That works both ways. Sometimes it's the girls who want to control the guys. Either way you have to figure out who you are and what's important to you."

"I suppose. I'm not sure I know who I am or what I'm feeling."

"No one fully does at sixteen." Sometimes not at fifty-five, not even when you'd thought you had it all together.

"Sometimes I wish no guys liked me, so I didn't have to even think about dating," Lizzie said.

"Have you tried talking to your dad about your emotions? Sometimes parents are more in tune than you think."

"Maybe a cool parent like you, but not my dad. He thinks I'm a kid and not a very smart one at that. Everything I do is wrong."

"It may seem that way to you at times, but I'm sure he loves you very much. He just worries about you."

"It doesn't feel that way. Sometimes I think he hates me."

"He may have trouble relating to you, but I'm sure he doesn't hate you. Why would he?"

"I was only nine years old when I caused my mother's and grandfather's deaths. Not literally, but Mom, Grandpa and Grams were on the way to see my dance recital when a drunk driver in an SUV swerved into our lane and crushed them against a bridge railing."

Carolina stood and put an arm around Lizzie's shoulders. "Oh, sweetheart, what a terrible thing for you to go through. I know it was traumatic for you, but it certainly wasn't your fault. I'm sure your father doesn't blame you for that, and you must never blame yourself."

"All I know is our life changed after that.

Dad practically became a zombie. Sometimes we'd be sitting in the living room, not talking or anything, but when he looked at me I'd see tears in his eyes."

"I'm sure your father was heartbroken. I know I was when my husband died. Grief can rob all your happiness for a while, sometimes for a very long time. But that doesn't mean he blamed you, not even subconsciously. You have to talk to him about this."

"I was thinking that maybe I could talk to Dr. Otis, you know, as a patient."

"I think that would be an excellent idea."

"Would you talk to Dad about it for me? I'm afraid he'll just start badgering me with questions about what's wrong and things will only get worse."

"I'll talk to him."

"Thanks."

Lizzie was dealing with far more than Carolina had realized. Counseling could be beneficial, but Lizzie might not be the only one who needed it. The problems she had with her father had been brewing for a long time.

Her conversation with Lizzie had accomplished at least one thing. She knew what she and Jake would be talking about that afternoon.

Chapter Eleven

The early-afternoon sun was searing into Thad's back, burning right through the thin cotton of his T-shirt. He took a shortcut through a maze of tombstones, wilted flower arrangements and cheap plastic remembrances.

He had come here often at first, when the pain had still bled into the thrill of the kill. This was the first time he'd been here in years. He wasn't exactly sure where the poorly marked grave was now.

But he'd find it, the same way he'd found the information he needed last night when he searched through the confusing maze of the internet.

The rancher's name was Jake Dalton. He lived with his mother and his teenage daughter. That information had been easy to discover after Thad had followed Jake, Mildred and Carolina to the Silver Spur Ranch.

Actually, he'd followed them from the time they'd left the hotel. Mildred had ridden in the front seat beside the rancher as they drove around Austin in his fancy black truck. They'd lingered for over an hour at an Italian restaurant and then gone shopping as if she'd never given another thought to responding to his text.

There would be no more texts. He'd dropped that phone from an overpass into the Colorado River. Even if his lying, cheating ex-wife wanted to get in touch with him, it was too late now.

Mildred had squandered her chance to do this peacefully, but that didn't mean she wouldn't have to pay for her sins. And once they were across the border, there would be no interfering bitch like Carolina Lambert for her to run to, crying for help.

There would be no Carolina Lambert anywhere—at least not alive. He could almost taste the sweetness of his revenge. For four years, he'd planned how he'd kill her. Each step of her murder was indelibly etched in his mind as if it had happened a hundred times before.

She thought she was on top of the world. He would drag her into a bottomless pit of shame and degradation. Her body would be ravaged, her dignity trampled. And then finally, when she was too destroyed to even beg for mercy, he'd put his hands around her neck and squeeze until her face turned blue and her body went limp.

He closed his eyes and let the ecstasy flow through him.

The ringing of his new, untraceable cell phone shattered the moment. There was no caller ID, but he didn't have to wonder who was calling.

The only man who had this number was his former prison mate Mateo Salinas. Adrenaline shot through Thad's veins as if it had been injected with a giant needle.

"What's up?"

"Your first job for the man."

He hadn't expected this to come so soon. "What kind of job?"

"There's a female border-control agent in Brownsville who needs to be taught a lesson and made into an example."

"You want me to kill her?"

"No. Want her alive so she can tell people who was responsible for the beating. Just beat the bitch up real good, whatever kind of torture turns you on. I know that's your style. But make sure she knows it's not a random act but what happens when you mess with the cartel."

"This bitch got a name?"

"Melissa Green. She lives alone, but there's

a guy who hangs out at her house a lot. He drives a red, souped-up '92 Mustang convertible. Make sure his car isn't there when you make your move. And be aware, she has a weapon and won't hesitate to use it if you give her the chance."

A gun changed the odds. "I could get shot."

"You want a job or not?"

He didn't have a lot of choice. It would be way too risky for him to stay in the country once he'd whacked Carolina. "I want the job— as long as you keep your word to get me across the border safely."

"I told you. The boss takes care of the ones who take care of him. Get the job done. Then contact me immediately. We'll have only a few hours to sneak you over the border before every law enforcement officer in Texas is on your tail."

"All I have to do is rough her up?"

"Put the hurt on her big-time. Mess this job up and I never heard of you. I don't protect men I never heard of. Get the picture?"

"Got it. There won't be any screwups on my end, but like I told you back in the clinker, there will be two of us crossing the border."

"Fine. Bring your own poison. I don't give a damn who you share your bed with, but there will be plenty of senoritas when you're craving fun."

"I may need a few more days."

"No problem." Mateo laughed as if they'd shared a hilarious joke. "Take all the time you need, long as the job's done by midnight Sunday. Maybe sooner if the boss says so. Whatever the boss says goes."

Thad's hands knotted into fists, anticipation running hot inside him as the pressure swelled in his brain.

Killing Carolina was now on countdown.

But first he had to tell someone goodbye.

Chapter Twelve

Carolina dismounted when Jake did, without waiting for his help. Touching his hand to the butt of his holstered pistol, he scanned the area before leading the horses to drink from a spring-fed creek.

It was next to impossible that Caffey would show up out here. But if trouble of any kind came calling, Jake was ready for it.

He turned his attention back to Carolina, who was already making the rocky climb to the nearby ledge. Even with unsteady footing, she was graceful.

Not surprisingly, she had demonstrated that same skill in the saddle. Self-assured, confident, trusting the horse he'd picked for her, she'd kept up with him easily as he'd taken Riley from a trot to a full gallop.

When they reached the open range, she'd

urged her horse faster, looking back only once to make sure Jake was following.

He'd taken advantage of the view. Her hair had caught the wind, dancing behind her, trapping rays of sunshine and casting them off like ribbons of gold. Her back straight, her head high, her long legs hugging the saddle, she'd looked positively regal.

Leading the horses back to the shade, Jake tethered them to the low-hanging branch of a sycamore tree and hurried to catch up with Carolina.

"First time to ride?" he teased.

"First time today." She smiled and did a 360-degree turn, slow enough to soak in the scenery. "It's beautiful here."

"Not the best view on the ranch, but it's close."

"The Bent Pine is beautiful, too, but in a different way. More pines. Not totally flat terrain, but it doesn't rival this."

"Every part of Texas has its own charm," he said, "but the Hill Country is my favorite. The Big Bend area runs a close second, though."

Carolina nodded her agreement. "We used to camp out there when my sons were much younger. To my mind some of the best hiking trails in the world."

The path grew steeper, the rocks beneath

their feet less stable. Jake reached for her hand to help steady her. She took it, her fingers curling around his. A perfect fit.

The crazy dizzying attraction hit again. Nothing he could adequately describe but somewhere between watching the birth of a new foal and getting kicked in the gut by a bull.

He struggled to ignore it. He hadn't asked her to go riding to seduce her.

Or had he? Was his libido ruling his subconscious?

"You must love the Silver Spur," Carolina said.

"Always have," he admitted, "since the day Mom married for the second time. I was on top of the world the day we moved into the big house. I got not only a dad I loved but a ranch to live on."

"My husband used to say that ranching wasn't an occupation, that it was a calling and that the love of it seeped into your blood."

"I get the feeling you think the same. A good thing I guess since you own one of the largest and most productive ranches in the state."

"I do love the Bent Pine, but I don't actually own it. My link to the land is strictly bound by heartstrings."

That surprised him. "Is that how your late husband framed the will?"

"No, but everything would have eventually gone to my three sons, so I made the decision a few years back to give them full legal possession of Lambert, Incorporated, which includes the ranch, the oil company and its subsidiaries."

"Sounds a little risky to me. You must have a lot of faith in them not to fear they'd lose it all through bad business decisions or perhaps even sell it."

"They won't do, either. They're honest, hardworking and savvy. And they love the ranch as much as I do or more."

And ownership apparently meant little to her. Which made his first assumptions about her encouraging a will that would lead to her eventual acquisition of the Dry Gulch Ranch even more ludicrous.

The last few yards to the top of the ledge were the steepest of all, the trail narrowing so that they were forced to go single file. Even so, she didn't let go of his hand until they reached the top.

"Wow! What a view," she said.

"Worth the climb?"

"Absolutely."

The top of the ledge was fairly flat before falling off again on the other side. Jake took a seat on a large rock with smooth edges.

Carolina found a rock of her own. "Did you invite me riding today to show me this?"

"Not entirely."

"So why did you invite me?"

A weak moment. A need to find out if she was genuine. An attempt to find something about her he didn't like. All were at least partially true but nothing he was willing to share with her.

"With all that's been going on over the past three days, I thought we should at least have a chance to talk one-on-one," Jake said. "I also figured you could use a break. Nothing like a good ride to soothe the mind and soul."

"It worked, to a point," she admitted. "I wouldn't say I'm completely soothed, but I'm glad we're having this chance to talk."

"So what advice do you have for me from Dr. Otis?"

"Nothing from Dr. Otis, but I would like to talk about Lizzie."

"What about her?"

"I had lunch with her today. I was sitting by myself and she walked over to join me."

"Did she tell you I'm an overbearing ogre who's cramping her lifestyle?"

"No, it's a bit more serious than that."

His mind went off on a tangent. Serious like being dragged into trouble by that hoodlum he'd forbidden her to see? Taking drugs? Pregnant. He reined in his fears. This was his Lizzie they were talking about.

He gulped in a lungful of air. "How serious?"

"She's dealing with a lot of emotional issues, Jake. She was impressed with Dr. Otis today and thinks he could help her deal with them."

Jake found that difficult to believe. "Lizzie is volunteering to see a shrink?"

"Yes. She asked me to talk to you about the possibility of private counseling."

His spirits plummeted. So this was what it had come to. His own daughter felt she had to have an ally to deal with him.

He buried his head in his hands. "I try. I really try, Carolina, but she turns away from me or gives me that eye roll to suggest I'm irrelevant. I guess the truth is I'm a lousy father."

"You're not a lousy father. Lousy fathers don't worry the way you have, the way you're doing right now. But from what she said, it seems the problems between you go back a long way."

"How far?"

"To the death of her mother."

He muttered a curse beneath his breath. That was the last place he'd wanted to go today. "What did she tell you?"

"I don't want to betray her confidence," Carolina said. "Besides, the issues have to be dealt with between the two of you, possibly with Dr. Otis's intervention."

"I probably wasn't the help I should have been to Lizzie at the time of Gloria's death. I was barely holding on to sanity myself. I'm sure I made bad decisions."

"Grief does that, especially in the early stages. But a child of nine has even fewer coping mechanisms."

"Lizzie amazed everyone at the time with how well she handled everything. I guess she kept the real hurt buried inside."

Carolina put a hand on his shoulder. "Lizzie is amazing, Jake. I'm sure she was then, too. But she still has issues that need to be faced, and she still needs you."

He stood and walked to the edge of the ledge. His whole world stretched in front of him. A few minutes ago the serene, pastoral landscape had made him feel on top of the world. Now he felt as if the huge rock he'd been sitting on was resting on his shoulders.

"Don't beat yourself up about this, Jake. It's not that unusual for teenage girls to go through a rocky period, even ones who haven't lost their mothers. Luckily she has you and her grandmother to center her world with love, even though she might not see it that way now."

"I hate the prospect of having a shrink crawling around inside my head digging up the past, but if it's what Lizzie needs, I have no choice."

"In the long run, you won't be sorry. I can almost promise you that."

"You would have been a good psychiatrist yourself, Carolina Lambert."

"No way. I'd never be able to stay subjective. I'd jump headfirst into everyone's problems."

The way she had done with Mildred. The way she was doing now with Lizzie. The way she was doing with R.J.

Jake had misjudged her seven ways to Sunday. She really was the kind to want to step in and rescue a neighbor with no thought of what she would gain from it.

"I'm sorry I put such a damper on our beautiful outing," Carolina said.

"Me, too," he admitted honestly. "You know how we cowboys are. We're tough enough to face angry bulls and untamed stallions, but throw in an emotional factor and it scares the wits out of us."

"You're tough enough, Jake. I have no doubt of that."

"Thanks for that vote of confidence."

"We should get started back," Carolina said. "Your mother will be arriving soon, and I don't want her mad at me if you're not there to welcome her home."

"About that, I need you to do me a favor when you're with her."

"What kind of favor?"

"Don't mention Thad Caffey to her, and ask Mildred not to mention him, either. I'll tell her about the situation if need be, but I don't want to get into it on her first night back."

"That makes sense."

"And don't mention R.J. to her."

"What if she brings him up?"

"She won't."

Neither of them spoke as they made their way back down to the waiting horses. Today hadn't worked out as planned. But at least Carolina had left him with a possible route back to his daughter.

"Same time tomorrow?" he asked as he helped her mount. "Only without the psychology session."

"It's a date."

In that case, he'd bring wine.

"You should have seen him after I poked that cone of gelato in his face. He was standing there sputtering like crazy, ice cream dripping from his mustache and a strawberry stuck to the end of his nose. My friend Katherine was laughing so hard, she swore she peed in her pants."

Lizzie reached across the table and gave her grandmother a high five. "Way to handle a pickpocket."

Carolina wasn't about to wet her panties, but she couldn't remember when she'd laughed harder or enjoyed an evening more. Mary had fascinated them with tales of their European adventures and had them in stitches over some of their misadventures.

"I'd like to travel with your group," Carolina said, "except I don't know if I have the energy to keep up with you."

"Sure you can. Just get you a cane like I carry. People give me a wide path. Guess they figure if they don't get out of my way, they might get tripped or clobbered with it."

"Tell me you don't go around tripping people who get in your way," Jake said.

Mary's eyes twinkled, lighting up her smile. "Hardly ever."

Jake shook his head. "I don't want to go on a trip with you. I'd probably end up in jail."

"Anyone for more dessert or another cup of decaf?" Mildred asked.

"None for me," Mary said. "It's past my bedtime, or at least I think it is. Hard to tell with that jet lag playing havoc with my body clock."

"If you're tired, it's bedtime," Jake said. "I'll walk you back to your room to say good-night."

"No, I'd like Carolina to walk me back to my room. We should get to know each other better."

"You're back a day and I'm already replaced."

"Temporarily. Besides, I have a cane that Carolina might want to borrow in case you get too bossy."

Everyone stood when Mary did. She was like a beloved queen in a way. After knowing her for only a few hours, Carolina could understand why.

She was joyous to be around and didn't hesitate to say what she was thinking. She must have been a good match for R.J.'s stubbornness. No wonder their marriage hadn't lasted.

Mary made her way around the table, giving Mildred a warm hug and hugging and kissing both Jake and Lizzie on the cheek. The house was much more like a home with Mary around.

Mary linked her arm with Carolina's as they walked to her first-floor suite. It was at the far end of the hall, past Jake's office.

When she opened the door, Carolina breathed in the faint odor of lavender.

"I'm glad you're here," Mary said. "You're good for my son."

Oh, no. Somehow she'd gotten the wrong idea about her and Jake. "I'm only here for a few days. Jake is letting us use the Silver Spur for the Saddle-Up charity project."

"I know, dear. He told me. But that doesn't change the fact that you're good for him."

"Thank you, Mary. He's also good for me."

She hadn't realized how true that was until the words slipped from her lips.

But she was only here until Sunday.

IT WAS AFTER ten when Carolina finally climbed between the sheets. Her body was tired, but her mind was churning. Tomorrow's Saddle-Up activities, her talk with Lizzie, Mary's words— and Jake.

Their relationship had become a conundrum. She wasn't sure exactly what she felt for him, but it was nothing like what she'd experienced with any other man since Hugh's death almost five years ago.

She'd liked riding with him today. When he took her hand, awareness had hummed inside her. When she'd had to tell him about Lizzie and witnessed his pain, it was all she could do not to wrap her arms around him.

She shouldn't feel any of those things. She'd loved Hugh with all her heart. How could she think of any other man as more than a friend?

Her cell phone vibrated. She didn't recognize the number on the caller ID. A rush of dread swept through. *Please don't let it be Thad Caffey causing more trouble.*

"Hello."

"Is this Carolina Lambert?" A woman's whispered voice.

"Yes. Who's calling?"

"It doesn't matter. I just need to warn you."

"About what?"

"Thad Caffey. He's planning to kill you soon. You need to go away somewhere he can't find you."

"What makes you think he is going to kill me?"

"He said so. Not to me. He didn't see me. When I heard him talking, I hid. But I heard him tell his sister, Jane, that he was going to kill you. I couldn't live with myself without letting you know."

"Is that all he said?"

"I have to go now. But he means it. He's killed before, you know?"

She hadn't known. She still didn't. This could be some cruel hoax perpetrated by Thad. "Who did he kill?"

The connection went dead. Carolina hit call back. The phone rang. And rang. And rang. No one answered.

She shivered and pulled the coverlet over her.

She would not let Thad Caffey get to her. She was safe here.

She'd tell Jake about the call in the morning and call Sheriff Garcia, as well, but she wouldn't let Thad's threats control her life.

With luck he'd be back in prison where he belonged in a matter of days or even hours.

Get ready for that, sister Jane.

Chapter Thirteen

Jake paced his small office, so angry he could barely make sense of what Carolina was saying. "Go get Mildred. We need to get to the bottom of this."

"I don't think she's even out of bed yet."

"It's seven o'clock. Go wake her," he insisted.

"Isn't there any way we can leave her out of this?" Carolina pleaded. "When I've asked about Thad's life before they married, she's never seemed to know much."

"If she knows anything, I want to hear it."

"I guess you're right." Carolina stopped to pick up their two empty coffee cups from the corner of his desk. "I'll be right back—with Mildred and more caffeine."

The fact that Thad Caffey wanted Carolina dead wasn't a shocker. Nor was the notion that Caffey was capable of murder. This might even be the lead they needed for the police to find and arrest him. The coward might still be hanging out with the mystery sister, Jane, bragging on what he planned to do while waiting on the chance to catch Carolina alone.

It was the fact that Carolina had to deal with any of this that made Jake's blood boil. He was not a violent man, but if he'd known Monday at the capitol what he knew now, he wasn't sure he could have kept from beating the son of a bitch to a pulp. Not that Jake's going to jail would have helped anything.

But he was damn tired of that two-bit criminal calling the shots. It was time for action. He was still pacing and considering his next move when Carolina returned with Mildred ten minutes later.

"I should have left the second he confronted us Monday," Mildred said. "I'm so sorry about this."

"I only told her I'd received a threat by phone from an unknown source," Carolina said.

"Good. Forget the recriminations, Mildred. I didn't call you in here to blame you," Jake said. "I just need some facts about Caffey's family."

"Of course. I'll tell you anything I know, but that won't be much. As far as I know, it was just him, his mother and a sister."

"A sister named Jane?"

"Yes. How did you know?"

"The caller mentioned her. Do you know where Jane lives?"

"She's dead. She was murdered several years before we were married. Thad did tell me that much."

That added a twist. "Who killed her?"

"No one was ever arrested for the crime. Thad didn't talk about her much. When I asked about his family, he'd get upset, so I would just let the subject drop. I got the impression he and Jane were very close."

"But you're sure she was murdered?" Carolina asked.

"I'm sure he told me that. I never knew anything for sure with Thad. He lied to me more than once, sometimes about things that didn't really matter. He'd just lie instead of admitting the truth."

"How old was she when she was murdered?"

"Nineteen. She was two years older than Thad. Like I said, he didn't talk about her much, but…"

"But what?" Jake coaxed.

"I think I reminded him of her. Sometimes he'd call me by her name without seeming to realize it. I feel weird even saying this, but sometimes he'd call out her name when we made love. That would really creep me out."

"That would creep anyone out," Carolina said. "Did you question him about that?"

"I did the first few times, but he'd deny that it had happened and say I was making things up to hurt him. I stopped asking after he slapped me across the face so hard my vision was blurred for hours."

And yet Mildred had stayed with Thad. Jake didn't get it, but then he'd never walked in Mildred's shoes.

"He sent me a huge bouquet of roses later that day to say he was sorry," Mildred added, almost as if she were still justifying his barbaric, abusive actions.

"You mentioned his mother," Jake said. "Did you ever meet her?"

"No. He said she was so upset over Jane's death that she died from a heart attack. I always thought the trauma of losing both of them was what made him so erratic.

"At least that's how I excused his behavior. The truth was that I was more afraid of being alone again than I was of living with him. It wasn't until Carolina got me hooked up with a counselor in Dallas that I was able to see that."

Carolina had a habit of saving people. A reminder that he'd have to be careful not to read too much into her being there for him and Lizzie.

"Where were they living when Jane was murdered?" Carolina asked.

"Gunshot, Texas. It's about a hundred miles west of Dallas, so small it's not even on most maps. West of nowhere and east of hell, Thad used to say. You only pass through it if you're lost. I wanted to visit there, just to see where he grew up, but he wouldn't go back."

East of hell, but close enough Thad could easily have driven there yesterday and talked to Jane—if her murder had been another of his lies.

Jake asked a few more questions Mildred couldn't answer. It might not have helped if she could, since there was no way of knowing how much Thad had told her was actually true.

But there were ways of finding out.

"Thanks for the help, Mildred."

"I just wish I knew more."

"You gave me a place to start," Jake said. "So now go out there and get those volunteers in shape."

"I'll do my best."

When she left, Carolina walked over and dropped into his chair. "I think we should call Sheriff Garcia and give him an update."

"Agree."

"And then we should take a drive to Gunshot, Texas, if we can find it."

"If it exists I can find it. But I want to do a little investigating before I go running off chasing after a woman named Jane who may be dead. But let's start with a phone call to Garcia and see where we go from there."

If he did go on a field trip to Gunshot, she was not going with him. He'd fight that battle when he came to it.

"WHERE IS THAT damn sock?"

It had been there a minute ago. Garcia scooted over to make sure he wasn't sitting on it and then shoved the top sheet back to see if it was entangled in the covers.

He would have thought it was a sign he was getting old if he hadn't been losing a shoe or a sock or a shirt he'd laid out ever since he became sheriff.

Too many problems cavorting about in his hard head. Too many nutcases out there with nothing to do but cause trouble. Song should have said "Mama, don't let your babies grow up to be criminals."

His phone started vibrating. He reached over to the bedside table to get it. It was hiding under the dad-burned sock. Maybe he was getting old.

He checked the caller ID. Had to be more trouble if Jake Dalton was calling this time of morning. "What's Caffey done now?" he answered, sure that the deadbeat thug was the reason for the call.

"Talking to the dead, from what we've heard so far."

"Likely can't find nobody else to talk to him. But you gotta be clearer than that for me to help you."

"Carolina got a phone call last night from an unidentified woman. I'll switch the phone to speaker and let her tell you about that."

"Nothing Caffey's up to would surprise me," Garcia said when Carolina finished with her story. "But he wasn't talking to his sister, Jane, any time lately. She's been dead for years."

"According to Mildred she was murdered," Jake said.

"That she was. Brutally murdered and her body left to be eaten by the buzzards. The prosecutor dug up that information while preparing his case against Caffey."

"And the killer was never apprehended?" Jake questioned.

"Nope."

"Do you know which detective investigated the murder?"

"Not off hand, but that's a rural area. I s'pect it was the sheriff's office that handled the investigation. But sometimes in a murder case like that, the Texas Rangers or one of the big-city police departments will be called in to help. The sheriff's name is Lonnie McDowd. He's been there a long time. He'll know how the case was handled."

"I'll give him a call."

"You can do that, but you might get more out of him if you talk to him personally, that is if you've a mind to get that involved."

"I've a mind to," Jake said.

"Then go face-to-face with him. Not that I'm recommending you get involved at all. There's a warrant out for Caffey, and I still s'pect him to be arrested any minute now. I'll let you know soon as that happens."

"We'd appreciate that," Carolina said.

"I reckon you've called your sons and told them about last night's phone call," Garcia said.

"No," Carolina admitted. "Tague is the only one on the ranch right now, and I'm sure he has his hands full running the Bent Pine. You agreed that I'm in good hands, so there's really no reason to bother him."

"He'd want to know."

"I'll be home on Sunday. I'll tell him all about it then."

"He's gonna blow a gasket when he finds out you waited so long to tell him."

"I'll give it some thought." Garcia figured that statement was to humor him. But he knew

Tague. He wouldn't take kindly to being left out of the loop where his momma was concerned.

Garcia would do what he thought was best. He was still the sheriff.

ONCE THE CALL was over, Carolina stood and walked to the door. "What time do we leave for Gunshot?"

She'd caught Jake off guard. "Did you forget that you have approximately thirty women showing up here in about two hours to partake of your expertise?"

"Not today."

News to him. "Did you cancel the training?"

"No, but today is devoted to team-building activities—a very important part of the campers' experience. We have a specialist coming in to teach the methods, and Sara and Mildred are coordinating the activities. They don't need me."

"Good. You need a day with fewer responsibilities. But you're still not going with me. It isn't safe or necessary."

"Sorry, Jake. I appreciate all you've done, but either I go with you or I go by myself. Your call."

Fear for her safety battled his admiration for her spunk. The fear won out. "The deal was that you stay on the Silver Spur until either Caffey is arrested or you return to the Bent Pine. But I promise that I'll share everything I learn with you when I get back."

"The deal was I don't leave the ranch alone. The question was when do we leave. It would work better for me if I have time to get the day's session started, but I can leave earlier if we need to."

Problem was he believed her when she said she'd go with him or go alone. Not a chance he was willing to take. "Let's shoot for ten."

She gave him a little salute as if he were in charge, though she'd just won the battle. She was the most independent, exasperating woman he'd ever met.

He'd keep her safe or die trying. No. He'd keep her safe and Thad Caffey was going back to prison. Hopefully Jake would get at least one good knockout punch to Caffey's gut in the process.

Now all he had to do was go explain all this to his mother and tell her that she was not to leave the ranch today without an escort just in case Caffey was in the area waiting to cause trouble.

Carolina had complicated his life to the max. Now he was forced to deal with two fiercely independent women before breakfast. And still he liked having her around.

GARCIA PADDED TO the kitchen, one sock on, one foot bare. He needed a shot of caffeine bad. He had faith that Jake Dalton could protect Carolina Lambert, and he had all the respect in the world for her. But he was friends with all her sons, too. Good men. Solid. Cowboys to the core.

Tague was the youngest of the three, funny, good-natured, seldom seen angry. But he'd get his dander up for sure if he found out his mama's life was being threatened and she hadn't told him anything about it.

Tague would be plenty riled at Garcia, too, if he found out he knew and didn't pass on that information. No need to get on the bad side of the Dalton men.

As soon as he got his coffee, he went back to the bedroom and finished getting dressed while he considered the risks in going against Carolina's wishes. He didn't even get the khaki shirt of his uniform fully buttoned before he'd made up his mind.

He sat back down on the edge of the bed and made the call.

SHERIFF MCDOWD LOOKED to be in his midsixties, going bald, needed a shave and to lose about fifty pounds. He leaned back in his desk chair and gave his whiskered chin a good rubbing.

"What can I do for you?"

"There was a woman named Jane Caffey murdered in Gunshot, Texas, several years back."

"Yep." He gave Jake and Carolina a good once-over. "Are you two in law enforcement?"

"No. I'm Jake Dalton. I have a ranch south of Austin. And this is Carolina Lambert."

McDowd clicked his tongue and gave Carolina another studious look. "You part of the Lambert Incorporated bunch?"

"I am."

"Thought you looked familiar. Now, what's your interest in the Caffey case?"

Jake explained the situation.

"So Thad Caffey finally went to prison. Good to know, even if he is out for the time being. You know he was the prime suspect in his sister's murder for a while."

"We had no idea," Carolina said. "What made them suspect him?"

"I don't remember the details. Neighbors reported him as strange, stuff like that, but no solid evidence. He was never arrested. No one was, so whoever killed her is still walking around a free man."

"Is there someone who might remember more?" Jake asked. "The lead investigator, maybe."

"Likely so. Donald Morgan handled that case.

He was retired from the FBI when he signed on with us. He'd been in profiling for years and had a real knack for it. He was convinced Thad was guilty. Like I said, he never found enough evidence to convict him. After Mrs. Caffey had her stroke, Thad quit school and left town. Never heard of again until now."

"I thought Thad's mother died of a heart attack a few days after his sister died," Carolina said.

"No, she had a stroke about a year after the murder. Lived a few months and then died of a heart attack while in a rehab center."

"Are you certain?" Carolina asked.

"It's the way I remember it, but Donald can tell you more. He followed that case for several years."

"Is Donald Morgan still with your department?" Carolina asked.

"No, he got shot in the leg two years ago trying to stop a crack-high thug who was robbing a liquor store. He retired for good then. Built himself a lake house on Lake Johnson. He and his wife moved up there, and I haven't seen him since."

Lake Johnson. In the Hill Country. Much closer to Austin than Gunshot was. "Do you have a number where I can reach him?" Jake asked.

"No, but I'll see if I can get it for you. I know one of my deputies has stayed in touch with him."

"I'd appreciate that, the sooner the better. Time is of the essence here."

"I get that. Leave me your card and I'll have him get in touch with you."

Jake pulled a Silver Spur Ranch card from his pocket and slid it onto McDowd's desk.

"One more question," Carolina said as they were getting up to leave. "Do you know where Jane was buried?"

"I reckon right there in Gunshot. There's an old cemetery there behind the remains of a Baptist church. Church hasn't been open for the soul-saving business in years, but I think they're still burying folks behind it."

"Thank you."

Jake didn't have to wonder where they were going next.

CAROLINA WALKED SLOWLY, admiring the remains of what must have once been a beautiful old country church. The highways and back roads of Texas were sprinkled with those, many still standing, still cradling the dreams of generations, though they'd weathered hurricanes, tornados, floods and fires.

This one had not fared nearly as well. The bones of the building were mostly bare, the wooden planks lying on the ground in rotting piles. A bell tower still reached to the sky, but the bell was missing and the cross that topped it was cracked.

Jake walked at her side, stopping when she did, often with a hand at the small of her back. She was growing comfortable with his touch. She wasn't sure if that was good or bad or even what it meant. For now, she was just thankful to have him with her. And for the fact that he was licensed to carry the pistol he'd just holstered at his right hip.

"It may take a while to find Jane's grave," Jake said.

She looked past the ruins to the row upon row of tombstones of every size and shape imaginable.

"Maybe they're in order by date of death."

"Doesn't look that way. I see bouquets of fresh flowers a few feet from a crumbling tombstone that looks like it's been there for a hundred years."

"Well, at least we have the place to ourselves."

"Just us and the ghosts."

"If you think you're going to frighten me out of searching for Jane's grave, you're mistaken."

"It was worth a try." He took her hand and they walked the maze together, occasionally stopping to read and smile at a humorous epitaph left on a tombstone. A few brought the quick burn of tears to Carolina's eyes.

"Only a few hundred left to go," she said after forty minutes of heat and humidity and swatting at honeybees and mosquitoes.

Jake took a handkerchief from his back pocket and wiped beads of sweat from his brow. "And then you owe me a beer."

"Icy cold," she said. "Plus lunch if you find the grave."

"Now, that's what I call incentive."

They were near a dirt road in the back west corner of the cemetery when she spotted it. Not a tombstone, but only a small cement marker that read Jane Dalton and the words Till Death Do Us Part, followed by the dates of her life span.

"Dead at nineteen," Carolina said. "Brutally murdered. So sad. Maybe Thad was perfectly normal before that and the trauma pushed him over the edge."

"You do like to look for the good in people. Personally I think it's more likely he beat her to death the way he almost killed Mildred."

"I don't deny that sounds plausible," she admitted.

"Do you think he's the one who came up with the epitaph? It doesn't read like something a brother would say about his sister."

"No," Carolina agreed, "but Mildred did say they were very close."

Carolina studied the other markers in the area. "I don't see her mother's grave. You'd think it would be nearby, since she died so soon after Jane."

"There's probably a story there, too. Hopefully not as depraved as Jane's murder."

Carolina jumped, startled by a rustle in the grass. She was immediately aware of Jake's hand flying to the butt of the pistol. Her heart jumped to her throat.

"Over there," Jake whispered, pointing to an elderly woman shuffling through a row of graves a few yards from them. A basket of blossoms swung from her arm.

She showed no sign of noticing them as she stopped and knelt at a grave. Scattering red and yellow peonies, she began to hum an old hymn that was one of Hugh's mother's favorites. Grams sang it often while she knitted.

Carolina turned to Jake. "Do you think she could have been the one who called me last night?"

"I'd say it's doubtful, but anything's possible at this point."

"I'm going over and talking to her."

"I'll go with you."

She shook her head. "I think she might be more receptive if I go alone."

To her relief he didn't argue the point, though she knew he'd be steadily scanning the area. He hadn't said it, but she knew he was as aware as she was that if Thad had been overheard talking to his sister's grave, he could still be in the area.

"Hello," Carolina called before getting too close so as not to startle her.

The woman looked up and smiled. "Hello. I didn't think anyone was around. There seldom is."

"I'm here with a friend."

The woman looked over to where Jake was standing. "Got yourself a cowboy. Mighty fine-looking one at that. Better hold on to him if he's as good as he looks."

"I'll tell him you said that. Your flowers are beautiful."

"Thank you. Charles loved working in the garden. I don't like it much myself. Too many bugs and too hard on my back. But I've managed to keep his peonies alive."

Carolina looked at the new tombstone. Charles had been dead for six months. "Was Charles your husband?"

"He was—my second husband. My first is

buried two rows over. He never liked peonies, but he grew lots of delicious vegetables. Both men as good as gold."

"Were you by any chance here yesterday?"

"I was, last night about dark. I come here often when my arthritis isn't misbehavin'." She pointed to the dirt road. "If you look down there, you can see the roof of my house."

"No wonder we didn't see your car. When you were here last night, did you see a man standing over by where my friend is right now?"

The woman didn't answer, but her face twisted into a frown, her loose skin tightening around her mouth but spilling over her chin. Carolina was sure that was fear shadowing her eyes.

"Don't be afraid. No one is going to hurt you. I'm Carolina Lambert. If you're the one who called me last night and warned me about Thad Caffey, I want to thank you."

The woman looked around, her gaze still fearful. "I called you. My son found your number for me on the internet somehow."

"Then you saw Thad Caffey in this cemetery last night?"

"And heard him, too. He was talking to his sister's grave like he thought she was still listening. Things he said he was going to do to you made me so sick I almost threw up in the grass."

"Did he see you?"

"No. He thought he was alone or he wouldn't have said such depraved things. I scrunched down behind that big tombstone just behind us and stayed hidden until he left."

"How did you know the man talking was Thad Caffey?"

"He called Jane his darling sister, and that was the only sister he had. He killed her, you know."

"How do you know that?"

"Everybody around here knows that except the police. If he hadn't left town when he did, somebody around here would have killed him and that's a fact."

"Then we'll pray he's gone for good this time," Carolina said. "Can we give you a ride back to your house?"

"No. I can use the exercise. But you stay close to your cowboy over there. He'll keep you safe. I can tell by the way he's watching over you now."

"I do believe you're right." Carolina gave her a quick hug and hurried back to where Jake was waiting.

"Let's get out of here," she said. "By the way, do you like peonies?"

"What are peonies?"

"Never mind. It's time to go get that beer."

Chapter Fourteen

They stopped at a backwoods diner a few miles off the interstate whose sign heralded the best catfish in Texas. Carolina had doubts about the claim's veracity, since dozens of eating establishments in the state made that same promise.

When the hostess welcomed them, Jake pointed out the table he wanted. It was in the far corner of the room, one that would offer plenty of privacy to discuss what they'd learned about Thad Caffey this morning.

Mainly it boiled down to the facts that Caffey had been a suspect at one time in the death of his sister and that he'd been back in his small rural town of Gunshot last night. Both facts had already been passed on to Sheriffs McDowd and Garcia.

Carolina excused herself to go to the restroom while Jake was being seated. By the time she returned, an amber-colored beer in an icy mug was waiting for her.

She took a sip and licked her lips. "You ordered well, cowboy."

"I thought you might like that. It's a Texas craft brew they carry on draft."

"Good choice, though the heat and humidity have me so parched, stump water might taste good."

"Maybe for an after-dinner drink."

He was doing his best to break the tension of the morning. Amazingly, it was helping.

She perused the menu and settled on a grilled-chicken salad. Jake ordered the fried fish. He was halfway through his beer before he leaned back in his chair and broke the easy silence that had settled between them.

"No offense intended, but you're a tough babe to be one of Texas's rich and famous socialites."

"I raised three Texas boys and was married to a man who was bigger than life. I had to be tough or be lost in the machismo."

"With me it's just the opposite. With Mom, Lizzie and Edna in the house, I have to feign a rugged masculinity to keep from having someone paint lipstick on me."

"You do a good job of feigning."

"Thanks."

"Tell me about your family," he said.

"You probably know the basics. I'm a widow and a grandmother with three sons, three grandchildren and another on the way. We own a ranch and Lambert Oil. That covers it."

"That's the surface. Tell me the good stuff. Who's your favorite daughter-in-law? Do you ever have big family brawls over who gets the chicken legs? Which grandchild do you spoil the most?"

"You do want the dirt. I truthfully don't have a favorite among my daughters-in-law. They're all special in their own ways and they make my sons very happy."

"Then tell me about the grandchildren you've spoiled rotten."

"They're not rotten, but not from lack of trying on my part. Belle, Emma and Damien's adopted daughter, is absolutely adorable and so cute you just want to hug her till she squeals. She's almost five. Their son, Zachary Hugh, is a toddler, into everything and gives the best kisses in the world.

"Then there's Tommy, Alexis and Tague's adopted son. He'll be in the first grade in September and already a cowboy at heart. He loves the rodeo and riding his pony. And he can climb like a monkey. He's on top of everything.

"And Meghan and Durk are expecting their

first child in October. I can't wait for another baby in the house. Did I leave anything out?"

"The chicken-leg fights, but I admit that is rather personal."

"No chicken-leg fights. An occasional riot over who gets the last bite of banana pudding or slice of chocolate cake, but that's as rough as it gets. Well, unless Aunt Pearl drinks the last of Grams's sherry. Then the fur—or at least Pearl's horrid black wig—has been known to fly."

"Do you all live on The Bent Pine?"

"Yes, but not all in the big house. We're a regular commune. Durk also has a high-rise condo in town for nights he has to work late or any of the family wants to stay over in Dallas for the theater or a ball game. Then there's Grams, my late husband's mother, and her widowed sister, Aunt Pearl. Never a dull moment."

"Sounds like you have it all."

She'd thought so, or as much as she could hope for after losing Hugh. Surely it was still true, but there was something about being with Jake that made her realize for the first time what she'd missed by not having a man in her life.

Not just for sex, but for moments like this— quiet talk and sharing a beer. Like the touch of his hand on the small of her back or his hand reaching out for hers.

Like the way he was looking at her right now, as if he could devour her but still he didn't push for more.

By the time the waitress brought their food, her insides were quaking. Was all the craziness with Thad Caffey making her delusional? Or was it possible she was actually falling hard for Jake Dalton?

LIZZIE TOOK THE steps two at a time and swung through the back door. She'd figured losing driving privileges would totally ruin her summer, but today had been really fun. She couldn't wait to help with the team-building games when she was a junior counselor. The heat she could do without.

The air conditioner felt heavenly. She gulped in the cool air and tugged her sweaty shirt away from her body. She'd planned to head straight for the shower, but odors wafting in from the kitchen waylaid her.

Edna was pulling a sheet of snickerdoodles from the oven.

"How was your day?" Edna asked without turning to see who was there.

"Good. How did you know it was me?"

"The smell. You need a shower, young lady."

"And cookies. I need energy. I'm a working girl now."

"I'll wrap some in a napkin for you to take with you, but you wash your hands before you eat them."

"Naturally. Do you know where Mrs. Lambert is? She didn't show up for the training session today. I asked Mildred about her, but she just said Mrs. Lambert had some business to take care of."

"She went somewhere with your dad. They didn't say where they were going, but your dad said he'd call if they weren't going to be home for dinner, so I expect them anytime now."

"Mrs. Lambert and Dad. That's weird." Lizzie wondered if they'd talked about her seeing Dr. Otis. She didn't think her dad would be mad, but he'd want to talk it out and that never got them anywhere.

"Where's Grandma?" Lizzie asked.

"She said she was going back to her room for a nap a couple of hours ago. I haven't seen her since. I reckon it's the jet lag making her so tired in the middle of the day and the napping all afternoon that keeps her from sleeping through the night."

"Okay. I'll see her later. Off to shower."

"Use lots of soap."

"I know and wash behind my ears. I'm not three." She nabbed a cookie from the napkin, stuffing half of it in her mouth as she raced up the stairs.

When she got to her room, she grabbed another cookie and checked her cell phone. Ten missed calls from Calvin. He'd be steaming she hadn't called him back, but Mildred had stressed no phone calls except emergencies during team building.

Her phone started to vibrate. Him again. Ignoring his call, she shimmied out of her jean shorts and kicked them and her shoes into the corner. He'd waited all day; he could wait until she'd showered.

He was only going to growl at her anyway.

The phone was ringing again when she got out of the shower. She wrapped herself in a towel and tied another turban style around her hair.

Eleven phone calls. Maybe he'd had an emergency. A wreck on his motorbike or been arrested. A surge of guilt sent her flying across the room.

"Hello," she said breathlessly.

"Where have you been all day?"

"Working. I told you I'm training to be a junior camp counselor."

"Oh yeah, that. Well, you should have called me. It happened."

"What happened?"

"I'm getting sent to live with my dad. Not that you'll miss me. You'll be off camping."

"I'll miss you, but I'll bet you'll be back before school starts."

"Nah. I'm not coming back, not staying there, either. I'm heading off on my own."

"You can't just run away."

"Sure I can. Thousands of kids do it every year."

"It's dangerous."

"I can take care of myself. Anyway, I just called to say goodbye. I plan to be gone in the morning before Mother wakes up."

She couldn't let him do this, not without at least trying to talk him out of it. Even Dad would understand that. Some things were more important than rules and grounding.

"Do you want to meet for a few minutes at our usual place?" she asked.

"Aren't you scared of your dad?"

"Not scared, but I don't like getting in trouble."

"Does that mean you want to meet me or not?" he quipped.

"I do. In fifteen minutes. But I can't stay long, and if you're not there I can't wait."

"I'll be there."

She hung up the phone and threw on some clothes. All the better if she could get there and back before her father got home. But if she didn't, she'd just have to hope he understood— and then be grounded for life.

THAD CAFFEY SLOWED as he reached the gate of the Silver Spur. It was the second time he'd driven by in the past thirty minutes, but time was running out and he was tired of waiting.

He'd made up his mind. It wasn't the way he'd planned things, but he could live without Mildred. As Mateo had said, there would be plenty of available señoritas once he got to Mexico.

But he couldn't leave without getting even with Carolina Lambert. It had been gnawing at his guts for four years. He'd lived on thoughts of what he'd do to her, how she'd scream for mercy. All she would get was justice. No one wronged him like that and lived to tell about it.

No one. Not even his Jane.

Thad was practically to the gate when he saw a car approaching it from the other side. The driver had long hair and sunglasses. The venom of revenge rushed through Thad's veins.

The gate opened and the car sped through it. He only got a quick glimpse, but it was enough to know that the female behind the wheel wasn't Carolina. He followed close behind and then passed slowly.

The driver looked right at him as he passed.

She was young, around the age of Jake Dalton's teenage daughter.

Adrenaline rushed through his blood at a murderous pace. Carolina would never turn down a cry for help from a teenage girl.

He might have just accidentally found the way to get Carolina to come rushing into his trap.

LIZZIE STARED BACK at the driver of the blue sedan as he stayed even with her instead of passing. At first she thought he must be someone she knew. Few people drove this back road whom she didn't know.

She didn't recognize him, and the way he glared at her freaked her out.

Finally he sped past. She breathed easier—but only for a minute or two. Once they'd crossed the bridge over Cotter's Creek, he slowed to a crawl. She slowed down, too. Whatever crazy game he was playing was dangerous.

Driving at ten miles an hour, she still caught up with him. She'd have to pass him and pray he didn't chase after her. She might be able to outrun him on a straight stretch, but there were blind hills and dangerous curves ahead.

Still, she had to pass. She put on her blinker. He stuck a hand out his open window and gave her a thumbs-up, as if she'd joined his treacherous antics. She was starting to get really scared. If this was what breaking her dad's rules came to, she was never breaking another one.

She fumbled in the side pocket of her tote bag for her cell phone. The blue sedan began to weave. The driver had to be drunk or high.

Suddenly he threw on his brakes. She swerved around him, missing him by inches. Her heart pounded in her chest. The cell phone slipped from her fingers. She leaned over and tried to retrieve it, but it had fallen between the seats.

She hit the gas. Her only hope was to get away from him. In seconds the blue sedan was in the wrong lane, driving even with her, so close she could have reached out and touched it. He swerved closer, scraping her brand-new car and ripping her side mirror from its bearings. The mirror dangled precariously, bouncing against the sides of the car.

He was going to run her off the road. Panic swelled inside her until she could barely breathe.

His car raked hers again, harder this time, the metal making a crunching noise that hammered in her ears. She lost control and had to steer frantically to keep from skidding off the shoulder and into a ditch.

She slowed as she fought to get the car back on the road.

Please just let him drive away. If she got out of this alive, she'd never break her dad's rules again.

The sedan slammed into her again, this time hitting the left fender so hard the car spun fully out of control. She held on to the wheel and braced for the ditch.

Instead the car rolled along the grassy area just off the shoulder until it sputtered to a stop. Smoke was pouring out from under the crinkled hood and through the vents. She had to get out before the car caught fire and blew up with her in it.

She struggled with the seat belt. It wouldn't budge.

Someone was beating on the door of her car, but when she looked up, all she could see was smoke.

She opened her mouth and screamed. She wanted her daddy. But Daddy was nowhere around.

Chapter Fifteen

The car door flew open. Coughing and struggling for oxygen through the smoky haze, Lizzie instinctively tried to shove away the man who was trying to pull her from behind the wheel.

She spotted the knife through her clouded peripheral vision. She tried to squirm away as he struck with it. Expecting pain, she shuddered with relief as the seat belt gave way and the man pulled her toward him. Her feet hit the ground.

She tried to break loose and run, but the man swept her into his arms like a bag of groceries and started running away from the smoking car.

"Are you okay?"

No. How could she be? The man's arms were holding her tight, and she was too dizzy and nauseated to even try to escape. The smell of smoke was still stringent, her throat dry and choking, but nothing like what it had been in-side the car.

"Take deep breaths," the man coaxed. "You're going to be okay. Just relax and breathe. I've got you and I'm calling 911 now."

Lizzie's eyes burned and watered as she heard him requesting emergency help, firefighters and an ambulance. She blinked repeatedly until she finally gained focus. She began to shake un-controllably.

The man holding her in his arms was not the leering lunatic who'd run her off the road. He was the hottest, hunkiest cowboy she'd ever seen in her life. She was hallucinating. Maybe dead.

Only he was much too real to be an illusion. Her mind cleared fast. "My car. It's on fire. I have to save it."

"Too late for that, but firefighters might get here in time to put out the fire before the car explodes and sets someone's pastures on fire."

"My dad is going to kill me."

"I promise you he won't, sweetheart. When he finds out what happened out here, he's just going to be thankful you're alive." He put her down, holding on to her until she was steady. "Now, are you sure you're okay? Nothing hurt-ing? Nothing bleeding?"

"My knee," she said, realizing for the first

time it was aching. "I must have banged it against something when the other car knocked me off the road."

He bent over for a closer look. "It's red, but the skin isn't broken. Guess I should introduce myself. I'm Tague Lambert."

"Lambert? Are you kin to Carolina?"

"She's my mother. Who are you?"

"Lizzie Dalton. I'm Jake Dalton's daughter. Your mother is staying at our ranch, the Silver Spur. Did you come here to see her?"

"I did. Good timing, if I do say so myself."

"Yeah, if you hadn't come along when you did, I might be dead."

"We don't even want to go there."

Lizzie looked around. They were standing next to a white pickup truck that must belong to Tague. Lizzie's car was on the other side of the road and several yards back. It was still smoking, but not as bad as it had been when the car first hit her. The blue sedan was no-where in sight.

"I saw the crash," Tague said. "It looked as if that blue Honda intentionally ran you off the road?"

"It did. The driver had been messing with me ever since I left the ranch. If I slowed down, he slowed down. If I sped up, he'd catch up, pass me and then slow down again. He sideswiped me once before slamming into my fender. Thankfully we weren't going very fast when he hit me."

"Road rage?"

"No. If it was, I didn't do anything to cause it. He just started following me."

"And you have no idea who he was?"

She shook her head. "I'm pretty sure he's not from around here."

"Did you get a good look at him?"

"Very good. I think I'd know that face and the slithering snake tattoo on his arm anywhere."

Approaching sirens screamed in the distance. Within minutes, a fire truck sped up to the smoking car.

One of the firemen rushed over to them. "Anyone trapped in the car?"

"No," Tague answered.

"Positive?"

"Positive," Lizzie assured them. "I was in the car alone, and Tague pulled me out before he even called you."

"Good man." The fireman looked back to Lizzie. "Are you injured?"

"Just a bruised knee."

An ambulance arrived and pulled off the road in front of her car. The firemen already had the blaze under control.

"Forget the gurney," the fireman said, waving the paramedics over.

Deputies from the sheriff's department were the next to arrive. Lizzie was starting to feel guilty that she wasn't hurt, since she'd caused all this commotion.

Over it all, she heard the familiar knock and growl of Calvin's motorbike. With all that was going on, she'd forgotten all about meeting him. He slowed when he passed, looked her right in the eye but didn't even acknowledge her. He just kept on going.

He no doubt figured he had enough problems of his own without getting bogged down in hers. But you'd think he'd have at least stopped to make sure she was okay. Some tough guy he'd turned out to be.

And this was all because of him.

Well, actually it was the fault of the lunatic in the blue car, but Lizzie wouldn't have been here if it wasn't for Calvin.

The paramedics began insisting she should go to a hospital and get checked out. She assured them over and over that she was fine. The deputies wanted her story but kept interrupting for details she couldn't give them.

"I can give you the license number of the blue Honda that ran her off the road," Tauge said.

All the attention turned to him.

And then a new vehicle joined the circus. Jake and Carolina had arrived on the scene. Lizzie's heart sank as the real truth settled in.

She was definitely going to be grounded for life.

CAROLINA STOOD ON the front porch, staring down the road that led to the gate, wondering what was taking Jake and Tague so long. The men had waited around to get the damaged car towed, but how long could that take? She'd driven Lizzie back in Tague's truck almost two hours ago.

Tague had saved Lizzie's life, appearing on the scene totally unexpected at exactly the right moment. It wasn't the first time Tague had been a hero. He'd met his wife when he saved her son from a carjacker. It was the first time Carolina had put him in a situation that required his heroism.

When they'd talked at the accident scene, it was clear Tague was agitated to have to hear about a credible threat on her life from Sheriff Garcia.

He'd made the drive from Oak Grove to see and hear firsthand what was going on and take her home with him, if necessary. He wouldn't have to do any convincing with that. She'd done enough damage here.

All she could think about was what if Tague hadn't driven up when he did? What if… She shuddered. The what-ifs were too scary to think about.

Carolina was certain from Lizzie's description that Thad was the man who'd forced her off the road. Since she was the one Caffey was out to kill, she was the one who needed to leave the Silver Spur immediately.

Mildred could stay here, and with Peg and Sue's help they could finish the training without Carolina. Her belongings were already packed.

Carolina had come here thinking that working with Jake would be next to impossible, a vexation to be endured. She would leave knowing that she would miss him far more than she would have ever dreamed.

All her previous perceptions of him had been wrong. Instead of being heartless, he was generous, honest, strong, loving and funny. She felt safe with him.

Carolina didn't understand his reluctance to reconcile with R.J., but he must have his reasons. She just wished he'd change his mind about them.

She was just about to go inside and see if she could help with dinner preparation when she spotted Jake's truck, kicking up dust on the road to the house. She walked down the steps to meet them, wondering how the two men had got along after she and Lizzie left.

Jake reached out to her, taking her hand and squeezing it hard. The contact felt good, natural, reassuring after the trouble she'd caused.

They dropped hands after that, but she was sure Tague had noticed.

"How's Lizzie?" Jake asked.

"Physically, she seems fine except for a bruised knee. Emotionally, she's a bit of a wreck and has every right to be. She talked a mile a minute when we first got here, telling her grandmother, Mildred and Edna every detail. She was even more descriptive than she'd been with us."

"How did Mom take it?" Jake asked.

"Great at first, but then she wiped tears from her eyes and we all started crying. Therapeutic for all of us. That was followed by lots of hugs, and then Lizzie rushed off to her room to call her friend Angie."

"Guess there's no use trying to keep any of this quiet," Jake said. "It is what it is. All comes down to the facts that we've got to stop Thad Caffey and I owe Tague big-time."

"Glad to help, though like I said, I don't think Caffey had any intention of letting her die."

"How can you say that?" Carolina questioned. "She was trapped in a car that could easily have exploded."

"Let's talk about it inside," Jake said. "How about the three of us meet in my office as soon as I have a chance to say hello to Mom and check on Lizzie?"

"Works for me," Tague said. "Will give me a few minutes to wash up."

No one waited for Carolina's vote before rushing off. Perhaps they'd already decided it was best for her to go back to the Silver Spur and the meeting was to tell her.

The thought stung. It was one thing for her to decide to leave. It was another for Jake to want her to go.

Now she was being ridiculous. It wasn't as if they were romantically involved or even that she wanted to be.

But she did like him. She liked him a lot. It was a very scary admission.

CAROLINA WAS ALREADY waiting in Jake's office when Tague arrived.

"Nice setup," Tague said, dropping to the tan leather couch on the opposite wall from Jake's large oak desk. "I wouldn't mind an office like this in my house except that Alexis hates it when I take care of ranch business at night."

"I don't blame her. You need family time.

I probably should follow that advice myself," Jake said.

"What did you mean when you said you didn't think Thad would have let Lizzie die?" she asked Tague, getting back to the issues at hand.

"Thad jumped out of his car like he was in a big hurry and started running toward Lizzie's wrecked, smoking vehicle. I can't imagine him rushing to get her out of a car that looked like it might explode any second if he was just planning to kill her."

"But he didn't rescue her," Carolina argued.

"No. Once he saw me he got scared and took off like he had a rocket under his hood."

"And you rushed to the car that could have exploded any second."

"Any decent man would have done the same."

She wasn't so sure of that. "Then why do you think Thad ran her off the road?"

"Maybe to use her as bait to get you to run to her rescue. Maybe just to scare you. Who knows what goes on in his sick little mind?"

Jake joined them in the room. "I plan to do everything I can to put him and his sick little mind back in prison where he belongs. I don't care what it takes."

"He must realize that," Carolina said. "Maybe he'll move on now."

"I doubt that," Tague said. "After hearing what he said at his sister's grave, he's obviously obsessed with getting revenge. But he did prove once again what a coward he is. He couldn't get away fast enough when he saw me get out of my truck."

"He'll wait until he can get Carolina alone," Jake said. "I'm almost sure of that, but I'm not taking any chances."

"I can see that," Tague said. "I came here to persuade Mom to come home with me, but I don't know that our ranch is any safer than the Silver Spur. At least here, she has the training session to keep her mind occupied with something other than a depraved maniac."

They were leaving out one very real concern, one that had just occurred to her. "If Thad came after Lizzie to get to me, what's to keep him from coming after someone in our family, Tague?"

"Me. I've already upped security at the Bent Pear and made sure everyone knows the new rules. I did that as soon as I got off the phone with Garcia this morning."

"The sheriff definitely didn't waste any time getting in touch with you."

"It was the right thing to do," Tague said.

"It certainly turned out that way," she agreed. "There's still the volunteers to consider. They have to drive the same back road for a few miles every morning to get to the Silver Spur. Some of them ride alone and unarmed."

Though she knew many did carry a weapon in their vehicle. Women in rural areas had been protecting themselves and their families from beasts for generations. This particular beast walked on two feet instead of four, but that wouldn't detract from their aim if they were threatened.

"I think you can forget about Caffey showing up out here again," Tague said. "He's whacko but not stupid. He has to figure local law enforcement will be on constant lookout for him."

"And if desperation and revenge rule, I still have it covered," Jake said. "I called a charter bus service while Tague and I were waiting for the tow truck to arrive. A coach driver will pick up the women at Carl's Diner on the interstate, a few miles from our exit. He'll chauffeur them to and from the ranch. Actually I should have thought of that sooner. It will save that backup at the gate every morning."

Jake and Tague had taken over with no input from her. But she still had a say.

"I've already made up my mind to cancel the rest of the training and go home," she said. "I've put you and your family out enough, Jake. You never signed on for this."

"I signed on to host the training session. It's not over."

"It is for me."

"What happened today was not your fault, Carolina. There's no reason for you to leave. Even Tague agrees with that."

"Don't you think you better ask the rest of your family how they feel about my staying?" Carolina asked.

"No, and it wouldn't change things if I did. No one wants you to go, Carolina." He stepped closer, his dark gaze mesmerizing. "No one."

She swallowed hard. How would she say no to that look?

"If that's settled, all we need now is an arrest," Tague said, breaking at least some of the fiery tension. "I figure that's only a matter of time. In the meantime, I'll keep in close touch."

"You may as well stay the night," Jake said, "or at least for dinner."

"No can do. We're inoculating cattle in the morning. I like to be home on the ranch to oversee that myself."

The men shook hands, and Jake thanked him again for jumping to Lizzie's rescue. It was surprising how well they'd bonded in one afternoon, almost as if they were old pals.

Carolina walked out with Tague.

"Am I picking up some romantic vibes between you and Jake?" he asked teasingly as they approached the truck.

A slow burn crept to her cheeks. "I have no idea what you mean by that."

He put an arm around her shoulders. "It's okay if you are, Mom. I'm not pushing, just saying it wouldn't bother Durk, Damien or me if you found someone."

She laughed and pushed him away. "Go home and don't worry about me or my love life." As if she had a love life.

He gave her a warm hug and kissed her on the cheek. "Me thinks you protest too much."

JAKE WAS ABOUT to go looking for Lizzie when she wandered into his office.

She walked over and perched on the corner of his desk, the way she used to do when she was a little girl and wanted him to stop what he was he doing and go outside with her. He hadn't done it often enough. Opportunities he could never regain.

"I'm really sorry about this afternoon, Dad."

"You should be. Do you know how much it scared me to see your car wrecked and surrounded by firemen and an ambulance?"

A stupid, rhetorical question. Of course she didn't know. Words couldn't begin to describe the hell he'd gone through in those few minutes until he knew she was safe.

"I shouldn't have broken your rules. I hadn't planned to, but then Calvin called and he was so upset about having to go live with his dad, I didn't know what to do."

"You could have called me."

"You would have said no."

"And you would have been safe."

"I didn't know there was some crazy guy stalking our gate. I thought everyone was worried about security because there were so many volunteers around or because Carolina is so famous. No one told me there had been a threat on her life."

"You were grounded. There was no reason to share those gory details with you."

"I know. I did everything wrong again. I do try, but I keep disappointing you."

None of the things he'd nagged her about seemed important now. All that mattered was that she was safe. All that mattered was that his heart hadn't been ripped from him again.

He had to find a way to bridge the gulf between them.

"Carolina told me that you want to see Dr. Olson as a patient," he said.

"I'd like to."

"I'll call him tomorrow and set up a couple of appointments. One for you and one for me."

"You're going. Why?"

"I've obviously made a lot of mistakes as a father. Whatever I'm doing wrong with you, I want to start doing right."

She walked around the desk, dropped into his lap and gave him a big hug. "I love you, Daddy."

Seconds later, she was gone.

His eyes were wet with tears when Carolina stuck her head in his door. He tried to whisk them away with his sleeve, but he didn't fool her.

"What's wrong?"

"Nothing." Nothing that wasn't better when she walked into the room.

"Then I guess we'd best go to dinner. Your mother said if you're not there in three minutes, she's starting without you. Said you know she hates it when her potatoes get cold."

"Queen Mary can wait."

Jake walked to the door, tugged Carolina inside and then kicked it shut behind her.

He wrapped his arms around her and slowly touched his lips to hers.

Chapter Sixteen

Carolina's heart leapt to her throat. She was being kissed. On the mouth. With passion. She hadn't even remembered what it felt like. Or that it could turn you inside out.

Right or wrong, desire flamed inside her.

Their breaths mingling, she sucked in the essence of Jake, reveling in the taste of his lips. She should pull away. But she couldn't. The need raging inside her was far too strong.

His hands tangled in her hair, his thumbs riding the column of her neck. Every part of her body responded as her breasts pushed against his chest. She couldn't reason and didn't want to. All she wanted to do was feel the sensations that were setting her on fire.

A knock on Jake's door broke the spell. She jumped away quickly, straightening her blouse, raking her fingers through her mussed hair.

"What do you need?" Jake asked. His voice was husky, almost gravelly.

"Dinner's ready," Lizzie called back. "And we can't find Carolina. Have you seen her?"

Carolina walked over and opened the door, praying the glow she felt inside wasn't showing on her face. "I'm here. We were just rehashing the day," she said. "But I'm starved. Let's eat."

She glanced back at Jake, half expecting him to look as changed as she felt. But it was the same Jake looking backing at her. Just a man. So why was he turning her life upside down? Why was desire strumming through every part of her body?

"Give me a minute to finish up something and I'll be right behind you," Jake said.

"Well, hurry. Grandma already said grace."

Carolina wondered if the minute he needed was to regroup after the kiss that had knocked her for a loop or if he was simply regretting it.

Was she regretting it?

Should she be regretting it?

Should she run as fast as she could from the primitive hunger that had driven her reaction to something as simple as a kiss?

She had never expected to feel that kind of passion with another man again. She'd given her heart so completely to Hugh. Was there enough left to build a new relationship?

A kiss, she reminded herself. Only a kiss, not a commitment.

It might mean nothing at all to Jake.

It WAS THE perfect summer night.

Katydids and tree frogs competing to see which could be the loudest. Nocturnal creatures rustling through the grass. Leaves fluttering in the breeze. The occasional haunting hoot of an owl. The eerie howl of a coyote. The creak of the front-porch swing as Carolina gently nudged it into movement with her foot.

Even the heavens were enchanting. The moon was a silver crescent, surrounded by stars so brilliant they looked as near as the fireflies darting in and out of the shrubbery that bordered the right side of the porch.

All sounds and sights that Carolina was so accustomed to that she seldom noticed them except on nights like this when her mind craved the familiar.

As familiar as home. But this was Jake's home, not hers. His world. His family. His past. Even if she wanted to, could she ever fit in here?

Once again she was jumping way ahead of herself, but she couldn't get the kiss out of her thoughts. For a few breathless minutes, desire had exploded inside her. A hunger so strong it had consumed her. An eruption of passion that she'd thought was lost to her forever.

The front door opened. To Carolina's surprise it was Mary who stepped out, her long white nightgown fluttering around her narrow ankles.

"I didn't realize anyone was out here," Mary said. "Would you mind a little company?"

"I'd love some company." Not completely true, but she scooted over to make room beside her in the swing. "I thought you went to bed a couple of hours ago."

"I did, but I woke up and couldn't get back to sleep. This old porch swing has soothed my worried mind on many a restless night."

"Jake said you've lived here since he was a young boy."

"Yes. We moved here when I married my second husband. I had no intention of ever marrying again after my divorce. Reuben gave forever a bad name. John made it a dream. Unfortunately, our forever ended much too soon."

"But you married again after your second husband died?"

"Yes. I've been married three times. That

makes me sound a bit risqué, doesn't it? I admit, I did like to have a good time back in the day."

"From what I hear, you still do," Carolina teased.

Mary chuckled. "So, how is Reuben doing—though I hear he goes by R.J. now?"

Carolina remembered Jake's warning and hesitated.

"You can talk about him to me," Mary said. "What happened between us happened a long time ago. The statute of limitations on divorce issues was reached an eternity ago."

"He's not doing well," Carolina said. "I heard from one of his daughters-in-law after dinner tonight. The doctor gives him another week or two at the most, but R.J. has fooled the doctors before."

"Is he still living at the Dry Gulch?" Mary asked.

"He is. The family plans to keep him there until the end."

"It's amazing that so many of his children reconnected with him after such bad beginnings."

"All of his children except Jake," Carolina said.

"Really?"

"Yes, even Jade, the daughter of a woman he'd never married. He'd offered, but Jade's mother turned him down."

"Smart woman."

Carolina hated to push the issue, but after all Mary had started this conversation. "Why do you think Jake refuses to take even a stab at getting to know his father?"

"That's between my son and R.J. You'll have to ask Jake that question."

Carolina had asked him, but she'd do it again. It would have to be soon. A few more days and it could be too late.

They talked a few more minutes, mostly about the Saddle-Up project, before Mary yawned and decided to try sleep again.

Carolina stayed—a mistake since it was the kiss that claimed her mind when she was alone again. She put her fingertips to her mouth. She could swear the heat from his kiss still lingered on her lips.

With a madman out to kill her, it was a kiss that would rob her of sleep tonight.

JAKE WOKE EARLY on Friday morning, as he always did. But running the ranch was no longer ruling his activity schedule. Thad Caffey and Carolina were.

Top of the list was to find Thad Caffey before he struck again. Jake had lain awake for hours last night, considering the facts and where he should go from there. He had a plan.

He'd stayed awake half the night thinking of Carolina, the taste of her, the flowery scent of her hair, the way she'd felt in his arms. He did not want her to walk out of his life on Sunday when she left the Silver Spur. He had no plan for how to ensure that.

He left the house at six, walked to the horse barn, saddled Riley and rode up to Cotter's Canyon. He'd come here daily when he first returned to the ranch after Gloria's death. The little solace he'd found he'd discovered here.

He slowed Riley to a walk. The horse easily maneuvered the rocky trail. A doe stepped out of a wooded area. It stopped and stared at Jake with its big brown eyes, then walked into the clearing. Two spotted fawns joined her, and they went about foraging for their food as if they knew Jake presented no danger.

Jake didn't stay long. The canyon seemed to have lost all its ability to clear his mind. By seven he was in the headquarters office making a call to a bounty hunter named Brad Pacer who'd made a name for himself in the Austin area locating missing persons who didn't want to be found.

The phone rang six times before it was answered.

"This better be damned important if you're calling this time of the morning."

"A matter of life and death," Jake answered.

"Then my help must be worth a lot of cash to you. Who am I talking to?"

"Jake Dalton. I'll pay you what you're worth, a whole lot more if I get quick results."

"Start talking, Jake Dalton."

Jake explained the situation.

"So all you want from me is to find this Thad Caffey, whose whereabouts you know as of yesterday."

"You got it."

"My price is three thousand dollars plus expenses."

"Locate him in forty-eight hours and hold him until the cops get there to arrest him and I'll triple that fee."

"You got yourself a deal. Now tell me everything you know about Thad Caffey."

Jake filled him in. "I'm also trying to get in touch with a retired law officer who lives in the Lake Johnson area named Donald Morgan."

"Formerly an FBI profiler?"

"That's the man."

"A friend of mine. I can give you his phone number now. You got a pen handy?"

"In my hand."

When they finished the conversation, Jake checked off hiring a private eye and obtaining

Donald Morgan's phone number from his list of urgents.

His next call was to Donald Morgan. His greeting was much friendlier. As soon as Jake mentioned Thad Caffey, Morgan became extremely cooperative. Jake made an appointment to meet with him at a coffee shop in Marble Falls at eleven o'clock. Check off item number three.

Before he could leave the office, he got a call from Sheriff Garcia, who obviously thought of him now as the contact person for all things dealing with Caffey.

"Good morning, Sheriff. Hope you're calling with some good news for a change."

"I have information, some obtained from your local sheriff's department. I don't know that it's particularly good. In fact, you may have already heard it."

"No. I haven't talked to anyone from the sheriff's department this morning."

"It turns out the blue sedan that ran your daughter off the road yesterday was stolen from a retirement home in Austin."

"That figures," Jake said. "He no doubt assumed he could outrun little old men in their walkers if they came after him."

"I've seen some who would give him a run for the money. But the rest of the story is that the stolen car was abandoned in a parking lot in Austin last night."

"Then they should have fingerprints to prove it was Thad who was responsible for the hit-and-run."

"They also have film from a security camera," Garcia said. "We should end up with at worst a grainy image of whoever parked and left the car. And I have the fingerprint report from the Oak Grove burglary on my desk this morning."

"Is it a match with Caffey?"

"It is. We have more than enough evidence to arrest him and make it stick. All we have to do is find him."

"About that, I want to offer a reward of ten thousand dollars for any information leading to his arrest and capture."

"That's a mighty steep reward considering we'll likely have Caffey under arrest in the next day or two."

"Every minute he's out there looking for a way to get to Carolina is a minute too long."

"It's your money."

"Right." But there was still one thing that didn't quite add up. "Why do you suppose he's not worried about leaving fingerprints and getting caught on camera? Is it possible he wants to go back to prison?"

"Makes more sense to think he's planning on disappearing, likely across the border."

As soon as he got his revenge. But the way he was leaving tracks, he must know his time was running out. He'd strike soon and go to any extreme to exact his revenge against Carolina.

The only way he could do that was over Jake's dead body. Jake had no intention of dying just when he had a chance at starting to really live again.

Chapter Seventeen

Thad Caffey had gotten the word. The assignment had changed. The saucy little border-patrol agent named Melissa was to be left bleeding and in agonizing pain sometime within the next twenty-four hours. The time range was nonnegotiable. She was off duty tonight and should be at home alone.

Caffey picked up the bottle of whiskey he'd bought with his last few dollars. He didn't like the taste of whiskey. Had never cared for any kind of alcohol. It was the drink of the devil. It had made Thad's mother beat him when he was little and kneel on rice until he cried.

He put the lip of the bottle to his mouth and swigged, letting the burn eat its way to his stomach.

Jane had never drunk, either. She didn't have hardly any faults, not until that filthy-minded preacher had come to town. He'd put some kind of spell on her, made her turn against Thad and tell him to never touch her again.

The preacher was the reason Jane had turned against him, the same way the rich bitch Carolina Lambert was the reason Mildred had turned against him.

Ten years ago Thad had made a terrible mistake. He'd killed the wrong person. He wouldn't make that mistake again.

He picked up the whiskey bottle again.

One woman to assault and torture. Another to kill. Twenty-four hours to finish both jobs.

He threw the half-empty whiskey bottle against the wall of his dingy motel room. The devil's juice sprayed the walls like amber-colored blood.

Thad grabbed his shirt from the back of a chair and poked his arms through the sleeves. The shirt smelled of sweat from two days of wearing it in the humid heat. It didn't matter.

He'd buy new ones when he reached Mexico.

Chapter Eighteen

As soon as they got past the handshakes and introductions, Donald Miller jumped straight to the topic of Thad Caffey.

"I figured he'd killed his sister even before he'd answered my first question. After an hour I was sure. But come on in. I should at least offer you a cup of coffee before I get started on Thad Caffey."

"Sure, but don't worry about the coffee. It's information I'm after."

Jake had checked Morgan's credentials a bit more on the internet before driving out. He'd been a big-time FBI profiler, aiding in identifying several infamous serial cases in the Northeast.

Jake hadn't found any indication as to how Morgan had ended up working for a primarily rural sheriff's department in Texas. Probably a story there somewhere, but Jake was only interested in the topic of Thad Caffey this morning.

However he'd landed in the Lone Star State, Donald Morgan had retired well. This was not what Jake had pictured when Sheriff McDowd called it a lake house.

It was in a gated community of homes that probably started at around four hundred thousand and ranged upwards of several million. Morgan's looked to hit at least the half-million mark.

The retired detective led Jake straight through the den and kitchen to a glassed-in sunroom that extended across the back of the house.

"Fabulous view," Jake said, looking out over a well-manicured lawn that led down to a dock and an expanse of water that sparkled in the sun like diamonds.

"That's what sold us on the place. Sit down. Make yourself comfortable. How do you take your coffee?"

"Black but don't go to any trouble."

"No trouble. It's already made. Unless you'd like something stronger."

"Coffee's fine."

All he really wanted was to get back to the topic of Caffey. Information about his past might not help with what was going on today, but it was always wise to know your enemy. And identifying clues into what makes a madman tick seemed to be Morgan's specialty.

Morgan was back in a minute with the coffees. Jake had taken a chair. Morgan took a seat on the couch, kitty-corner from him.

"You're not in law enforcement," Morgan said, repeating what Jake had told him earlier on the phone. "So exactly how are you involved with Caffey?"

Jake filled him in from the beginning, starting with his imprisonment for the brutal attack on Mildred and finishing with the hit-and-run yesterday. Morgan listened without interruption, though his facial muscles seemed to grow more strained with each sentence.

"I hadn't heard he was out of prison," Morgan said. "I tried to put all my unresolved cases behind me when I retired. Had to find some way to sleep at night."

"I understand. I'd just like to know your impressions of Caffey. I'm not looking for anything specific, because I don't know what that would be. His weaknesses, his patterns of behavior. Anything to help us apprehend him before he gets to Carolina Lambert."

"She's in imminent danger," Morgan said. "Any guy who'd kill his sister and then later whack his own mother is capable of heinous crimes."

"I heard his mother died of a heart attack after suffering a stroke."

"That was the best the authorities could come up with. I never bought it. Caffey nursed a maddening mixture of love and hate for his mother."

"He told you that?"

"Not in those exact words, but it was obvious. One minute he'd vehemently defend his mother against any suggestion that she could have been implicit in her daughter's murder—not that she was ever a credible suspect. Five minutes later, Caffey would go off on her alcoholism and how cruel she was when she was drunk."

"There must have been an autopsy when Mrs. Caffey died."

"There was. The part about her dying of a heart attack brought on by damage from the stroke checked out. It's the stroke story I have my doubts about."

"Why is that?"

"Medical reports indicated the stroke was most likely bought on by a lack of oxygen to the brain."

"Such as suffocation might cause."

"You got it. Caffey called 911 at two in the morning reporting that he'd found his mother in her bed, blue in the face and not breathing. When the ambulance arrived, the paramedics were able to revive her."

"So he called too soon?"

"The end result would have been the same," Morgan said. "She never spoke again."

"So if your theory is right, he got away with murder."

"Got away with it twice."

"And only got four years in prison for almost making it three," Jake said, thinking aloud. "What do you know about Thad and Jane's relationship?"

Morgan leaned back and crossed a foot over one knee. "That's where things really get interesting. A hodgepodge of information from various family members, neighbors and school personnel painted a clear picture of Thad's dependence on Jane. I can't say it was incest, but they were unusually close, almost always together, frequently holding hands when they thought no one was watching."

"Did anyone speculate why they might be so close?" Jake asked.

"Reports from friends and neighbors suggested Jane was his protector from their abusive, alcoholic mother, who was rumored to have frequently switched her son, occasionally hard enough to leave welts and cuts on his body."

"People knew and did nothing to stop her from beating the crap out of her young son?"

"Several of his teachers reported it. According to the records, their complaints were followed up on by the state's social services department. Thad was seven when they received the first complaint, small for his age, quiet and withdrawn.

"Both Thad and Jane denied any cruel and unusual punishment to the social worker and Mother Dearest must have wised up and quit leaving bruises anywhere they'd show. The case was eventually dropped."

"Basically the same pattern of behavior Thad displayed when he was married to Mildred, only this time he was the one with the power. Like a vicious cycle," Jake said.

"Happens that way sometimes, but not always."

"You must also have a theory for what sent Thad into the rage that left Jane Caffey dead."

"Actually, I don't, which left us with no motive. Partner that with no solid evidence that he did it, and there was no case. But I was so sure he did it that I followed him for years after that. Not as closely after he moved to the Oak Grove area, but I wasn't surprised to read that he'd gone to prison for almost beating his wife to death. Too bad they didn't sentence him for life."

"I second that one," Jake said.

He'd got what he came for—information that

helped explain the monster Thad Caffey had become. What he didn't discover was how to stop him for good.

"At least we know Caffey's a coward who only attacks when the odds are greatly in his favor," Jake said.

"So far," Morgan agreed, "but don't count on that always being the case. If he's desperate enough, he'll take more chances. That appears to be what happened in his encounter with your daughter on a public road. The only way you can protect Carolina Lambert is to get him back behind bars or kill him."

"Both options look good to me at this point," Jake admitted.

"Just be careful. Never take anything for granted where he's concerned. Predictability can never be depended on when you're dealing with someone like Caffey."

That pretty much said it all. Ten minutes later, Jake was on the road and heading back to the Silver Spur with nothing solid in his pocket to lead him to Caffey and even more evidence of how dangerous he was.

He'd have to tell Carolina about his visit with Donald Morgan. She'd be furious that he'd gone without her, but she deserved to know Morgan's take on Thad Caffey.

It would be his first time alone with her since

they'd kissed. He didn't know what to expect from her, but he did know she'd kissed him back. Not any perfunctory gesture but a mind-numbing, electrifying kiss that had turned him into mush.

They'd missed their date to go horseback riding yesterday. He'd make up for that today with wine and cheese and some of those fresh raspberries he'd seen in the fridge this morning.

And hopefully they'd wash it down with kisses—or more.

But he wouldn't push and scare her away. He was falling hard, and he wasn't going to blow this if there was any way to give their relationship a chance.

THEY HAD RIDDEN a different route today, one that skirted acres of hay fields, and then meandered through a wooded area before they rode at full gallop across rolling pastures. They finally stopped at the bank of a shimmering pond where two deer were drinking.

The startled deer looked up and then quickly disappeared into the forested area beyond the pond.

Carolina took a few seconds to rein in the exhilaration she'd experienced riding with Jake before dismounting. There was no explaining the way he affected her. There was no denying it, either.

With all she had to deal with, it was Jake's kiss that had kept her awake until the wee hours of the morning. She was over fifty, a widow, sensible—a grandmother, for God's sake. She didn't become giddy from riding horses with a sexy cowboy. Didn't get weak-kneed from a man's touch, certainly didn't get heart palpitations from a kiss.

But then it had been years since she'd been kissed like that. Plenty of sweet kisses from her grandchildren. Frequent pecks on the cheeks from her sons. And that New Year's Eve when Gillian Casey had grabbed her and placed that disgusting, slobbering smack on her mouth.

Still, she had to get her emotions under control before she made a fool of herself over a man she hadn't even liked a few days ago.

She'd be going home in two more days. After that, she'd likely never see Jake again. Her life would go back to the predictable. In the meantime, she had to get her emotions under control.

Jake walked over as she dismounted, took her reins and tethered them to the branch of an oak tree whose roots crawled into the earth like knotty fingers.

"You were right," Carolina acknowledged. "The ride was just what I needed to get the kinks out of my body and mind. Usually these training sessions are busy but fun. Thad Caffey has made this one an ordeal."

"Yes, and unfortunately I need to bring him up again."

"If you're going to tell me about the car Thad was driving being stolen and then abandoned, I already know. One of the deputies who investigated Lizzie's incident called me today. After that, I called Garcia to be sure he knew. He did and also told me they'd verified Thad's fingerprints were at the scene of the gun burglary."

"That takes care of two issues."

"There's more?"

"I've offered a reward for information leading to Caffey's arrest."

"That the sheriff didn't tell me."

"I'd asked him not to. I wasn't sure how you'd react, and I thought it might be better coming from me."

"I think it's a great idea. Only I can't let you do it. I'm the one Thad Caffey wants dead. If any reward is paid, the Lamberts will pay it."

"Fine. You pay the ten thousand. I'm not getting into a money fight with you. Obviously, the Lamberts would win. But I'm not exactly on poverty row out here."

"I didn't mean it that way."

"Good. Then that's settled."

It wasn't with her. "Do you have any more bombs to drop on me?"

"I met with Donald Morgan today."

"Without even asking if I wanted to go with you?"

"You had obligations here."

He was right, of course, but he could have asked. If he thought one kiss gave him the right to run her life, he was mistaken. Her emotions took off on another roller-coaster ride, this time all downhill.

She turned and walked away, with no particular destination in mind. He caught up with her quickly. He reached for her hand but she jerked it away.

"What did you learn from Morgan?" she snapped. "Or do you think you have to protect me from that, too?"

He grabbed her wrist and this time didn't let go when she tried to pull away. "If my worst sin is protecting you, I can live with that. But protecting you from a crazed madman is all I'm doing. I'm not trying to usurp your independence. Not that I could if I wanted to."

He let go of her wrist and she stepped away. This time she only walked over and leaned against the spindly trunk of a young elm tree. She took a deep breath and exhaled slowly. She had to stop letting every interaction between them—good or bad—affect her so strongly.

"Tell me what you learned about Thad from Donald Morgan," she said, struggling to keep her voice calm.

"Okay. Let me warn you, it's ugly. But I know you can handle it," he added quickly.

Now he was pandering to her as if she were an unreasonable shrew. Not without reason, she reminded herself.

Jake went through the details quickly, not making judgment calls or dwelling on the gore. Even the filtered version of Thad's past was disturbing.

"That's about it," Jake said.

"Scary, but horribly sad, too. It's no wonder Thad turned into the monster he is now."

"Sad, but lots of children go through traumatic childhoods and end up decent, responsible, even loving adults. Thad Caffey chose violence, and now it's consumed him. His reign of terror has to stop."

"I know," she agreed. "But think how tragically twisted and evil his mind and soul have become if he actually killed his sister and his mother."

"Right now I'm having a hard time mustering any sympathy for the guy. What do you say to a pact not to mention Caffey's name for the duration of our outing?"

"An excellent idea, but I can't guarantee clearing him from my thoughts."

"I have a bottle of wine to help with that."

Wine with Jake; just the two of them in an idyllic setting. A seduction scenario that would almost surely lead to another kiss.

"I don't think that's a good idea."

"Why not? Are you afraid of me?"

"No, of course not."

"Then I'll open the wine." He walked back to where the horses were tethered and unloaded a saddlebag that she hadn't even noticed before.

She watched nervously as he spread a blanket over a carpet of pine straw and then pulled a bottle of wine and two crystal flutes from a padded carrier. Only he didn't stop there. He opened individual containers of crackers, raspberries and cheese.

"Is this the typical Jake Dalton entertainment package?"

"Nope. This is the cowboy way to taking a lady's mind off her problems. Well, this and letting her help shovel out the horse barn."

"Then I'm glad you decided to go this way." The humor helped, but her insides were already quaking. If she was smart, this should be where the cowgirl rode away.

She couldn't bring herself to do that.

She joined him on the blanket and took the glass of wine he held out to her. Their fingers brushed. A heated sensation swept from her head to her toes, leaving her giddy before she'd even sipped the wine.

He held his glass up for a toast. "To beautiful beginnings," he said.

She clinked her glass with his. She sipped slowly, afraid of where this was going even while desire had her all but unglued.

He picked up a raspberry and slipped it between her lips. She chewed and swallowed, but it was not raspberries she was craving.

He trailed his fingers down her arm and then back up again, letting them dance across her shoulder until his thumb massaged the nape of her neck.

He was going to kiss her. Once he did, she was going to lose all control. Fear overrode the passion that was burning inside her. She backed away.

"What's wrong now?" he asked, frustration deepening his voice.

"I'm not sure what's happening with us."

"I figured it was pretty clear that I'm crazy about you."

"I like you, too," she admitted. "But I don't see where this can go."

"It can go wherever we want it to. We don't have to rush. If you don't want to make love, if you don't even want me to kiss you yet, I can wait."

Make love. She hadn't even considered that. If his kiss had sent her into ecstasy, what would making love with him do? The idea of it was exciting—but scary.

She'd loved Hugh. She'd been certain she'd never become drunk on another man's nearness, become giddy at another man's touch. That she'd never hunger for another man's kiss. That she'd never ache to sleep in another man's arms.

This time she was the one who leaned in close and claimed Jake's lips with hers. And then she was lost in the thrill of it all.

JAKE WAS TAKING a cold shower back at the house, trying to tamp down the sexual drives that would never be satisfied with just kisses. He might never be satisfied. He couldn't even imagine getting enough of Carolina.

But was Carolina really ready for this, or was it the danger intensifying her feelings? When she was safe, would she back off, be hesitant to fall in love again?

He had to admit that until this week, he'd

never seriously considered falling madly in love again.

But at some point, you had to go on with your life. He'd reached that point as long as he could move on with Carolina. If she needed time, he'd give it to her, even though it would mean a lot of cold showers and sleepless nights.

His phone rang. He rinsed the soap from his hair and body, stepped out of the shower and grabbed a towel. Still dripping, he knotted the towel around his waist and dripped his way to the phone.

"Hello."

"Brad Pacer here."

"Great. Dare I hope you're calling with good news?"

"I don't have your man in hand, but I do have some credible sightings reported. Seems he's working his way down south, driving an old beat-up gray compact car. Don't have the make or a license plate number yet."

"How far south are we talking?"

"A few miles south of Corpus Christi. My guess is he's heading to the border. I alerted Border Patrol to keep an eye out for him, but they already had him on their watch list."

"You're sure these sightings are credible?"

"At least three of the four are. The last one was at a truck stop on Highway 77. I showed the waitress his mug shot and tried to explain how he looked now. She jumped in and described that snake tattoo exactly as you did."

"I find it hard to believe that Caffey is going to give up on getting to Carolina," Jake said. "So if he is planning to cross the border, it won't be for good. The bastard will just be waiting it out until he feels it's time to strike again."

"You could be right."

Which would leave the danger hanging over Carolina indefinitely.

"What's next?" Jake asked.

"I called the state police and let them know where he was last spotted," Pacer said.

"Did they even know there was a warrant out for his arrest?"

"They did after they looked it up. I wouldn't hold my breath waiting on them to arrest him, though. Considering what they deal with every day in the border towns, a threat and a hit-and-run is about as high on their priority list as stealing a box of Girl Scout cookies."

"I'm sure it is, but finding Caffey is on the top of my list. Do you need more men to get the job done?"

"Not at the moment," Pacer said. "I'll let you know if that changes."

"Keep me posted."

"Will do. One other question. Have you ever heard of Mateo Salinas?"

"Not that I recall. Why?"

"He was in prison with Thad Caffey. I questioned one of the guards who said Caffey and Salinas buddied up before Salinas was released."

"What's Salinas's claim to fame?" Jake asked.

"He's involved with a Mexican drug cartel. I'm thinking Caffey might be headed down south to join up with him. In the meantime, I don't think you need to worry about Caffey showing up at the Silver Spur."

If Pacer was right and Caffey had cleared out of the area for now, at least they had some breathing room. Not that Jake was planning to let up on any of the security measures they had in place.

But he would need to tell Carolina the news, which meant bringing up the fact that he'd also hired a bounty hunter without discussing it with her.

He'd soft-pedal it later, when they were alone—whenever that turned out to be. He started pacing. The knot worked loose and the thick terry towel slid to the floor. He kicked it aside and kept walking, arousal rearing its head again as a plan began to formulate in his mind. Too bad bedtime was still hours away.

Chapter Nineteen

Carolina dipped her fingers into the jar of lilac-scented body butter. With long strokes, she rubbed the moisturizing nourishment into her arms until it was absorbed completely, careful not to get a glob of it on her clean pink night-shirt. Creaming her whole body was a nightly routine she'd initiated years ago, having learned soon after marrying Hugh that spending too many hours in the hot Texas sun could wreak havoc on her skin.

The prospect of becoming a rancher's wife had been scary. She'd known nothing about cattle or horses. Had never even been close to a tractor, much less driven one.

Now she couldn't imagine living anywhere but on the Bent Pine Ranch. Her sons and their families were there. Her memories were there. Her heart was there.

Jake Dalton's life was here, in this house, on

the Silver Spur, raising his troubled daughter, managing his mother, who at eighty was clearly a handful. Spry, independent and delightful. Still sharp enough that nothing got past her.

Which meant she had probably sensed the sparks between Jake and Carolina, just as Tague had. Surprisingly the idea of her being romantically involved with another man hadn't seemed to bother Carolina's youngest son at all.

She screwed the top back on the rich cream and walked back into the bedroom, closing the bathroom door behind her. She climbed into the king-size bed and slid between the crisp sheets.

A bed in Jake's house. On Jake's ranch. With the taste of Jake's kisses still on her tongue. With a hunger growing inside her that she longed to satisfy with a man she barely knew. She was falling in love. She wouldn't even try to deny that anymore.

She just couldn't fathom where the relationship could go. She had her life. He had his.

She turned off the lamp, wrapped her hands around one of the three spare pillows and hugged it to her chest. She was sensible. Mature. Responsible. But even knowing the odds were stacked against them, even knowing that when she left on Sunday this infatuation would likely end for him, even having a madman who wanted her dead to deal with…

She still wished she were sleeping in Jake's arms tonight.

A tap on the door startled her but only for a second. It was probably Mildred with a last-minute question about tomorrow's schedule or just wanting to talk.

She flicked on the lamp. "Come in."

The door opened and Jake stepped in, dressed only in jeans and carrying an overflowing tray.

"What in the world are you bringing me?"

"Normalcy. A first movie date. Like people have who aren't dealing with a madman."

"It looks more like food and drink to me."

"Hot chocolate, popcorn, Edna's homemade oatmeal cookies and movies." He set the tray on the desk and tossed a half dozen movies onto the bed.

"It's ten o'clock," she cautioned.

"We don't have to watch all of them. I wanted you to have a choice."

"Lonesome Dove? Hangover? Die Hard? The Good, the Bad and the Ugly?"

"Well, you weren't expecting me to own chick flicks, were you?"

"Absolutely not." She shoved the pillow she'd been hugging behind her and propped herself up to a sitting position.

He handed her a cup of the chocolate. "What's your movie choice?"

She patted a spot on the bed next to her. "I'd rather talk."

"As long as it's not about Thad Caffey."

"Who?"

"Atta girl." He crawled into bed beside her, on top of the coverlet, still in his jeans. "What shall we talk about?"

She knew she was probably about to blow the moment, but they couldn't always just get lost in the physical. If this had a chance of going anywhere, they had to really get to know each other.

"Tell me about your past, your life as a surgeon, your life with Gloria."

Jake frowned, his whole demeanor changing. "Do we have to go there tonight?"

"We have to be able to go there if we're going to keep having movie dates. I'm not asking for your darkest or your most personal secrets. I just want to understand you better."

"I'm not a complicated man. I am what you see, Carolina. No pretenses. No lies."

"How did you and Gloria meet?" she asked, moving him along before the desire to be in his arms overpowered her need to talk.

"We were both freshmen at the University of Texas. She was the superior student, determined to be a doctor since she was a kid and taking her classes very seriously. I had no idea what I wanted to do with my life. I was there to party."

"Then you didn't always want to be a rancher?"

"I did when I was growing up. From the day Mother married John Dayton and we moved onto the Silver Spur, I considered myself a full-fledged cowboy."

"What changed that?"

"John was killed in a hay-baling accident when I was fifteen. In my mind John was my real father and always will be. With him gone, I found myself hating ranching.

"That might have passed except a couple of years later Mother remarried. Butch Dickens wasn't a bad man, but he wasn't my dad. Looking back, I probably didn't give him much reason to like me. At any rate, we clashed at every turn. I couldn't wait to leave home."

"That must have upset Mary."

"She took it in stride. I think she figured I had a lot of growing up to do and I'd do it better out on my own. And I'm sure it was a lot more peaceful around here with me gone."

"What made you decide to become a doctor?"

"Gloria. From the moment we met, things started falling into place for me. We both knew we were meant to be together. I worked my tail off. It was a champagne-guzzling day for everyone when we were both accepted into medical school."

"And both of you went on to become doctors. That's quite an accomplishment for a bona fide cowboy."

"You better know it. Gloria loved kids. Becoming a pediatrician was a natural for her. I had to search a little harder to find my niche."

"What finally made you decide to become a surgeon?"

"The idea of cutting out the diseased tissue and being done with it appealed to me. I chose general surgery. Figured I'd lose fewer patients on the operating table than the specialist surgeons. I liked saving patients. Was never good at telling someone they weren't going to make it. I never missed that part of being a doctor."

"What did you miss?"

He lay back, letting his head rest on a pillow as he stared at the ceiling. "I missed my life with Gloria. After the car accident, after she died, I couldn't go on as if life still had any meaning. Besides, Butch was dead and Mother was in a coma. They didn't give me much hope she'd ever come out of it. I came back to take care of the ranch. It was the only thing I had to hold on to."

"You had Lizzie."

"And she was the only bright spot in my life. I was so lost in my grief that I'm sure I didn't give her enough attention. I can't help wondering now if that is what's at the root of our current inability to connect."

"You'll have a chance to work that out with Dr. Otis," Carolina offered.

"I hope he helps."

"Even if Dr. Otis doesn't have all the answers, you'll find a way to reach Lizzie. I'm sure of it."

Jake rolled over on his side and propped himself on his left elbow so that he was facing her. "I don't want to lose you, Carolina. What we have together doesn't come along every day. You must know that."

"I can't replace Gloria, Jake. No one can."

"I don't expect you to, no more than I can replace Hugh. What we build together won't diminish what we shared with them. We'll carve out space in our hearts and minds for us. Shared moments that are ours alone. A favorite movie. A song that belongs to us. All I'm asking is a chance."

All she knew was that she'd be crazy to walk away without giving them both that chance. She rolled into his arms and kissed him. Tender at first, then wild with passion.

"Keep this up and we're never going to get to that movie," she murmured.

Jake picked up the movies and slid them onto the floor. "In that case, Carolina Lambert, we are wearing way too many clothes."

CAROLINA WOKE TO a sweet ache in her thighs and the sound of Jake's rhythmic breathing. One of his arms was thrown over her naked abdomen. One of his legs crossed hers.

She hadn't been dreaming. They had made love, more than once. She'd never imagined she'd find this kind of magic a second time in her life.

He stirred, his leg sliding up hers. Delicious desires danced through her again. But it was morning and she had a training session to conduct.

She tried to slide from the bed without waking him. Instead he pulled her into his arms, his body spooning hers. His erection pressed hard against her.

"I thought you were asleep," she said.

"I was. Now I'm awake. Wide awake."

"Good because you need to get up and go back to your room before someone realizes you slept in here with me last night."

"I was thinking maybe I'd just shout it from the rooftop."

"That would create a stir." She pushed him away, threw her legs over the side of the bed and pulled on the nightshirt that had ended up thrown over the lamp.

"I have an idea," he said. "Why go home on Sunday? Why not spend at least a few more days here? Or we could go away. Colorado's nice this time of year."

"I have a better idea," she said, speaking as the idea formed in her mind.

"Let's hear it."

"You go home with me for a few days. Meet my family."

"I think I might be able to handle that."

"We could stop off at the Dry Gulch for a few minutes. You could say hello to R.J."

He stretched out across the bed. "You're never going to let go of this until I do, are you?"

"I might if you tell me why you're so set against even talking to your father."

"In the first place, I don't consider him my father. More important, he let me and my mother down when she needed him most."

"When was that?"

Jake got out of bed, wiggled into his jeans and walked to the window. "She kept calling for Reuben when she was in the coma. It took a few days for me to realize she was talking about her first husband. It had been years since she'd even mentioned his name."

"Did you call R.J. and let him know?"

"I did better than that. I paid him a visit. He was so drunk he didn't even know who I was when he came to the door half dressed in the middle of the day."

Carolina couldn't begin to make excuses for R.J. He'd had his demons. Alcoholism had been one of the worst. But he'd changed. He'd found redemption. His body was giving up. His heart had turned to gold. "Did you try to talk to him?"

"No. A woman half his age came staggering down the hall wrapped in a dingy sheet. I left without saying another word. My mother came out of the coma sixteen days later. She never mentioned Reuben again, and I never told her what happened."

"I can understand how you feel, but I still think you should see him—for both your sakes."

"I don't need anything from him."

"Then what do you have to lose?"

"Okay, Carolina. You win. But I'm doing this for you, not R.J."

She walked over, stopped behind him and rested her head on his shoulder. She'd never felt closer to him than she did at this second. "Thank you."

He turned and pulled her into his arms. This time she didn't push him away.

JAKE STRETCHED HIS legs under Granger's small kitchen table and studied the printout his foreman had just handed him. "I don't see a charge for that new feed blend I ordered when I was in San Antonio last week."

"They haven't shipped it," Granger said.

"They promised immediate delivery. Check with them on Monday. If they don't have a good reason for the delay, cancel the order. I don't want to start doing business with a company if I can't depend on their word."

"I'll take care of it."

Jake scanned down a few inches. "Looks like Dan Stinson robbed me again with those tractor repairs."

"He swears that everything except the two-hundred-dollar labor charge went into the parts."

"He always does," Jake said. "He's the best tractor mechanic this side of Austin, though, and I can't afford to have that big John Deere sitting idle this time of the year."

"And Stinson knows it," Granger agreed.

Jake pushed back from the desk. "Everything else looks good to me."

"Lanky says the engine on the Yamaha

four-wheeler sounds like it's chewing rocks," Granger said.

"Have Tilson take a look at that on Monday. He's got an ear for those ATV engines. Better than those diagnostics they run at the shop."

"Will do."

Expenditures and ATVs. Jake was going through the motions but having a devil of a time wrapping his mind around anything to do with the ranch. Carolina claimed too many of his brain cells.

He'd been with other women since Gloria's death. Beautiful women. Successful women. Women who'd made it clear they'd like nothing better than to become Mrs. Jake Dalton.

He wouldn't say he'd never enjoyed being with them, but there were none he'd wanted to be with when the sun came up the following morning.

He could have stayed in bed with Carolina all day. He could see himself having lazy breakfasts with her on Saturday mornings in the future, lingering over coffee and then going back to bed and making love until noon.

He could see himself curled up beside her watching the movies they'd never gotten around to last night or even a chick flick. He could picture the two of them cuddled in front of a roaring fireplace on a frigid January night, or dancing in the moonlight beneath a star-studded sky.

He could see spending the rest of his life with her.

He'd only felt that way about one woman before. If you'd asked him last week, he'd have bet the ranch that kind of magic could never happen twice. He might well be the luckiest man on the planet.

"You ever think about getting married, Granger?"

"All the time. But then I think about it some more and decide against it."

"Why?"

"I've seen too many men who let wives wreck their lives. Want to go hunting? The little lady wants you to spend the weekend with the in-laws. Want to go fishing? Wifey wants you to work in the yard. Want to have sex? She has a headache. My dog, my horse and my pickup truck. And a few cold beers on Saturday night. That's as good as it gets."

"Sounds like you got your philosophy of life from a country song."

"You can do worse."

Jake was hoping for a whole lot better.

"I need to let you know that I'll be away Sunday night," he said.

"Leaving when the crew of women do?"

"About the same time, hopefully around three thirty tomorrow afternoon."

"So what about all this extra security we have in place? Want me to call the dogs off with the exit of Mrs. Lambert and those Saddle-Uppers?"

"No. Leave it in place until I give the word. I'd like at least two men watching the house at all times while I'm gone. Move Tilson into the house. He can stay in one of the guest suites."

"He's gonna lap up that luxury like a starving dog."

"That's okay, as long as Mother and Lizzie are safe."

"So Thad Caffey is still on the loose?"

Jake nodded. "For now. Hopefully not for long."

But the odds of his crossing the border to freedom grew greater every minute. Jake glanced at his watch. Almost ten. He'd expected to hear from Brad Pacer before this. If Brad was as good as his reputation, he should have found Caffey and turned him over to the police by now.

"Anything else you want me to take care of while you're gone?" Granger asked.

"Yourself. Don't do anything to aggravate that leg."

"I'm watching it. This hobbling is getting old fast."

"You can reach me by cell at any time," Jake said. "Don't hesitate to call, especially if it concerns Mother or Lizzie."

"I'll see they're watched over. Don't you worry none, boss man."

He'd stop worrying when Caffey was behind bars. He waited until he was back in his truck and then made a call to Brad Pacer. No answer. He left a message for Pacer to call him back.

And he still needed to tell Carolina about the bounty hunter. Last night had not been the opportune time.

He placed a call to Sheriff Garcia's private cell phone to see if he had any news on Caffey's whereabouts. He was about to break the connection when the sheriff finally answered.

"Damn, Jake. You must be psychic. I was about to call you."

"With good news?"

"Not good for a young woman in Brownsville, Texas. Thad Caffey struck again."

"I'm not following you."

"Melissa Green, a young Brownsville woman, had her house broken into in the wee hours of the morning. She was savagely attacked, beaten and kicked until she passed out.

She's in the hospital now, undergoing surgery for internal injuries."

"I know Caffey is capable of beating up women, but how did they tie Thad Caffey to Melissa Green?"

"It was all caught on a security camera that he obviously didn't see."

"And it's a quality image, clear enough that you're sure the attacker is Caffey?"

"That's the word I'm getting."

"Attacking a stranger has never been his modus operandi. He must have some connection to her, perhaps in his past, in Gunshot or maybe in prison."

"Possibly. She works for Homeland Security with Border Patrol. She's not talking yet. If she does, we may find out more."

"By if, do you mean she may not make it?" Jake asked.

"Her condition is listed as critical."

"Has Caffey been apprehended?"

"No, but Brownsville is crawling with cops searching for him. If he's there, they'll find him."

"And if they don't?"

"Then it's possible he's already escaped into Mexico and free to travel to all points south," Garcia said. "He won't have changed, but he may be someone else's problem and not ours."

Jake reminded him of the obvious. "We can never rule out his sneaking back into the country."

"If he does, and Melissa Green dies, he'll face murder charges. If she doesn't, he's still earned himself a return trip to prison."

When and if they caught him. As long as Caffey was free, Carolina would never be safe.

Jake hated to interrupt her, hated even more to tell her the sickening new developments. But he couldn't wait. If she or Mildred had ever heard of Melissa Green either directly from Caffey or during his trial, Jake needed to know now.

If Caffey had any ties with anyone in Brownsville, he needed to know that, too.

All he asked was one solid clue to lead to Caffey's arrest. One more miracle. And he needed it soon.

"THERE HAS TO be a tie between Thad and the assaulted woman," Carolina insisted, seething at Jake's revelation of Thad's latest horror. "I can't imagine he drove to Brownsville to attack a random woman."

"I agree," Jake said. "That's why I asked Lanky to bring you and Mildred to headquarters to meet me. I'm hoping one of you has heard of her before."

"The only Melissa I ever heard him mention was the clerk at the market," Mildred said. "That was just to complain that she held up the checkup line chatting with the customers."

"What about Brownsville?" Jake asked. "Did he have family or friends there that you know of?"

"Not that he ever mentioned to me," Mildred said. "Don't you think he was just in Brownsville to cross the border into Metamoros?"

"And may already have," Jake said. "But if he hasn't, then he's hiding out in the area. If we knew his ties to Melissa Green, it might help us track him down."

"And they're sure that it was Thad who attacked her?" Carolina asked. "Because this sounds a lot like the work of one of the drug cartels, payback against a border agent."

"Another possibility," Jake said. "Did he ever mention any prison mates with ties to a drug cartel?"

"I don't remember him ever mentioning but one friend in his letters."

"Do you remember his name?"

"Salinas. Give me a minute. Salinas Mata? No. That's not it."

"Maybe Mateo Salinas?" Jake offered.

"That sounds right. Thad was impressed with him. Said Mateo was going to get him a job when he got out of prison and that we'd be clearing out of Oak Grove for good. That was before I filed for divorce and he stopped writing."

"Do you know Mateo Salinas?" Carolina asked.

"No, but I've heard of him from a contact of mine," Jake said. "Apparently he is connected with a drug cartel."

"You have friends in low places," Carolina said.

"Actually the contact is a bounty hunter that I hired to find Caffey."

"You hired a bounty hunter without even talking to me about it. Is that even legal?"

"He's legal and licensed," Jake said. "A retired navy SEAL who has a reputation for getting his man. He doesn't arrest anyone. He just locates the guy and makes sure the police know where to find him."

"How long has he been looking for Caffey?"

"Since yesterday morning. He'd followed Caffey's trail to Corpus Christi yesterday and suspected he was heading to the border. I haven't heard from him since then."

"So it could be that he beat up the woman in exchange for Salinas giving him a job or at least helping him sneak across the border illegally," Carolina said.

She shivered as chills crept up her spine.

"That's why he didn't care if he left his prints. He was planning to kill me first, drive to Brownsville, attack Melissa Green and then it was adios, America."

"And there's a good chance he would have killed you if Jake hadn't convinced us to move to the ranch," Mildred said. "I can't believe I made excuses for Thad's violent behavior for three years, right up to the moment he attacked me the way he did Melissa Green."

"You were lucky you got out of that marriage with your life," Jake said.

"What about Melissa?" Carolina said. "Will she live?"

"Her condition is listed as critical."

"I'm glad you hired a bounty hunter," Carolina said. "I want to be in the courtroom when they sentence Thad Caffey to life in prison."

"So do I," Jake said. "So do I, but if he gets shot first, I can live just fine with that, too."

Chapter Twenty

It was an hour later before Brad Pacer returned Jake's call.

"Sorry to be so late getting back to you. I've been investigating in an area with no cell phone service."

"Where is that?"

"I can't give away trade secrets, but suffice it to say, it's a place where you'd never turn your back on anyone."

"Have you heard that Caffey brutally attacked a female border-patrol agent in Brownsville sometime during the night?"

"I didn't hear about it until it hit the morning news. I contacted my sources and that's when I went way undercover to investigate."

"What did you learn?" Jake asked.

"The attack was payback for her shooting one of the cartel members in a shootout along the

Rio Grande last month. Border Patrol claimed it was self-defense. The cartel called it murder."

"But you don't have any leads as to where Caffey is hiding out now?" Jake asked.

"It's almost certain he's across the border by now, not legally, of course. They would have been watching for him at the checkpoints. But the cartels run people across like cattle whenever it suits them. The only laws they follow are the ones they make."

"But it is possible he could still be hiding on the American side of the border," Jake said.

"It's possible," Pacer admitted. "I haven't run into evidence of that. Sounds like you're not ready for me to give up the search."

"I won't be ready to do that until Caffey is in jail or dead."

"If I work both sides of the border, my price triples."

"Not a problem. I just want results."

"Then you're in luck. When restrictions are off the table, I always get my man."

LIZZIE PLACED A plate of sliced tomatoes on the table Jake had set up on the wide back porch. "I can't believe you two are leaving tomorrow. It seems like you just got here."

"But I'll be seeing a lot of you when you're

a junior counselor," Mildred said. "I'll be helping Sara out."

"Fun. What about you, Carolina?"

"I'll be coordinating the camps in the Dallas area. They will keep me very busy, but you can always come visit me at the Bent Pine."

"Did you hear that, Dad?"

Jake flipped one of the steaks he was grilling a few feet away. "I heard. I figure we can work that out one day."

Mary joined them on the porch, a pitcher of icy lemonade in hand. "What are you two working out?"

"Lizzie's visiting Carolina's ranch."

Mary's eyebrows rose. "Tell me more."

"We don't know when yet."

"Before the end of summer," Carolina said.

Jake said nothing. For a man who wanted to shout their relationship from the rooftops, he'd suddenly become suspiciously silent.

"What about you, Jake?" she prodded. "Do you want to visit the ranch, too?"

"He never does fun stuff," Lizzie complained. "He works on the ranch, goes to meetings and reads thick, boring books with no story."

"It's called nonfiction," Jake said. "But I guess I may as well tell you all that I'm going to follow Carolina and Mildred back to Oak

Grove when they finish up the training session tomorrow."

"That's a surprise," Mary said. "And a long drive there and back, especially getting such a late start."

"I won't be driving back tomorrow night."

"Why not?" Lizzie asked. "I heard Dad say that Thad Caffey escaped into Mexico. You're not still in danger, are you, Carolina?"

"No, and thankfully neither are you. Thad Caffey is nowhere near here." No use to frighten her again. She'd been through enough.

"Are you planning to see R.J. while you're so close?" Mary asked.

Matter-of-fact and straightforward. Mary must have always been that way. She and R.J. were probably a wild match, but Mary didn't hate him. Clearly she hadn't discouraged Jake from talking to his father.

"Who's R.J.?" Lizzie questioned.

"R.J. was my first husband," Mary said. "He's your dad's father."

"I thought John Dalton who got killed baling hay was Dad's father. How many husbands did you have?"

"Only three, dear." Mary sat down beside Lizzie and patted her hand. "And only one at a time."

"If R.J. is my grandfather, why have I never heard of him?"

"I'll take care of this from here," Jake said. He moved the steaks from grill to platter and joined them at the table. "It was John Dayton, not Dalton, who was killed in the hay-baling accident. Mother left R.J. when I was very young. John was the only father I ever knew, so it's natural he's the one you heard me refer to as Dad."

"If I have another grandfather, I want to meet him."

Jake put a hand on Lizzie's shoulder. "He has brain cancer, sweetheart. He's dying. You don't want to see him like that."

"I don't want to wait until he's dead. Why can't I just go with you and Carolina tomorrow?"

Jake looked at Carolina. She nodded her approval.

"I don't think it's a good idea," Jake said, "but if you really want to meet him, you can go with us. Just remember, he's very ill. I don't expect him to recognize me or understand that you're his granddaughter."

"Sometimes he doesn't even recognize me, and we're very close friends," Carolina said, knowing Jake was right to prepare Lizzie for the worst.

"You know, I think I'll go, too," Mary said. "You don't mind, do you, Carolina?"

"No. The more the merrier."

Jake groaned.

Carolina smiled and gave one of Lizzie's hands a squeeze. R.J. wanted to get to know all his family. He might be about to get more than he'd bargained for. She just prayed he was alert enough to know that his oldest son was finally coming home—even if it was for only a day.

Chapter Twenty-One

"A spokesperson from the hospital just informed KRGV-TV that Melissa Green, the border-patrol agent who was brutally beaten in her home last night, has died from her injuries."

Thad reached for the nearest thing he could find. His fingers closed around the cheap lamp. He picked it up and threw it as hard as he could at the TV. The screen shattered. The sound went silent.

He'd screwed up. Mateo had warned him not to make a mistake. Melissa Green was not supposed to die. Mess up with Mateo's boss and you didn't live to do it twice.

Mateo and some guy he didn't know had picked him up after the attack and brought him out to this run-down mobile home so far from civilization that no one could find him, and he had no idea how to find his way out.

They'd brought him clean clothes. Brought

him fast-food hamburgers and a couple beers. Took the rifle he'd stolen back in Oak Grove. Would have taken the automatic pistol if they'd found it on him. And then they told him they'd be back for him when they had everything in place to sneak him across the border.

He'd thought he had it made. He hadn't given up on killing Carolina Lambert. He was only giving her a reprieve.

They'd come for him just like they said. Any minute now they'd come for him. But he would never see Mexico. He'd never even see another dawn.

He had to get out of here. If he kept walking he'd have to eventually come to a road or a house or a railroad track he could follow. He went to the kitchen, searched the drawers and came up with a jagged-edge hunting knife, a screwdriver and an ice pick. It never hurt to have more than one weapon.

He'd never used an ice pick to kill and torture a woman. He'd never thought of it as a weapon—until now. The perfect weapon to plunge through the center of Carolina's heart.

He wouldn't get to Mexico, but he would get his revenge.

Chapter Twenty-Two

R.J. sat in his favorite chair and tried to keep up with the conversation going on around him. One-on-one, he could communicate with his sons, but when they all four got to talking together, it was just too dadgum confusing.

Adam walked over and stood by the arm of R.J.'s chair. "Do you remember who's coming to see you tonight?"

"Dog me if I don't. You done told me enough times. Jake outta be here by now. Do you think he got lost?"

"Carolina's with him, Dad. I'm sure she didn't get lost coming here."

"Probably had to hog-tie him to get him here," R.J. said.

"I doubt that," Cannon said. "More likely she used her womanly wiles."

Carolina and Jake. Be something if they were a couple. He'd always thought it would be nice if one of his sons ended up with her. Not that he didn't love the daughters-in-law he had.

But Jake was a widower with a teenage daughter. He needed a wife. He was about the right age for Carolina, too.

But R.J. wasn't sure Jake was good enough for her. He'd know after they talked unless he fell into one of those confusing spells where he had trouble even remembering where he was.

"Jake's mother is coming, too," Leif said. "And so is his daughter."

"You done told me that a dozen times, too."

"Sorry about that," Leif said. "You know how I tend to repeat myself."

"Do you remember Jake's mother?" Travis asked.

"Hell yes, I remember her. I fell in love with that prissy girl back in high school. Of course, every other boy in school did, too."

"But you were the one who ended up with her," Travis said.

"I dated her our senior year. I didn't end up with her. You don't see her around here anywhere, do you?"

"Not yet," Cannon admitted. "Did you two marry right out of high school?"

"Lands no. That girl wasn't even thinking about settling down. She couldn't wait to go away to college. She begged me to go with her, but I barely passed high school. Besides, Daddy needed my help running the ranch."

"Well, you had to get together at some point," Cannon said. "You married her."

"You guys are worse than a bunch of cackling hens."

"How did the two of you get back together?" Cannon asked.

"Best I remember, she just showed up back in Oak Grove one day. Got tired of living in New York, I s'pect."

"She sounds like an interesting woman," Adam said.

"She was that."

But those days were long gone. It was Jake he was interested in seeing now. He couldn't make things right with Jake. He'd been a terrible father and that was a fact. The drinking and gambling had taken him down. Nobody's fault but his own.

But he could say he was sorry.

R.J.'s eyelids felt heavy. He was getting sleepy. "Reckon they changed their mind about coming," R.J. said.

"They'll be here in a few minutes. Carolina would have called if there had been a change of plans."

R.J. got up and walked back to the kitchen for a glass of water. He took a glass from the cupboard and held it under the faucet. The water filled his glass and ran over his fingers. The water just kept coming.

The room started to spin. Faster and faster. He stumbled to the table and fell into a chair.

"Gwen," he called again. "Gwen. I can't turn off the water."

Gwen didn't come. She was never here when he needed her. There was something he was supposed to do tonight. He put his head on the table and floated away.

JAKE STOPPED IN front of R.J.'s house. Three pickup trucks and one car were parked in the driveway. Carolina was certain they were all eager for Jake and R.J. to get together.

"It looks like a party," Jake said.

"No one but the Dalton brothers are supposed to be here tonight," Carolina said. "And Brit and the baby. She and Cannon live in the house with R.J. The others have their own cabins scattered about the ranch."

"A grandfather, uncles, aunts and cousins by the dozens," Lizzie said. "I can't wait to meet everybody."

"Not this trip," Jake said. "This is to meet your grandfather. We won't be staying long enough for a family reunion."

They got out of the car. Carolina led the entourage with Lizzie right beside her. Jake and Mary brought up the rear. Carolina's nerves were on edge. She so wanted this to go well.

R.J.'s son Adam met them at the door and then led them to the family room for introductions.

Carolina looked around. "Where's R.J.?"

"He was in here and looking forward to seeing you until about ten minutes ago," Cannon said. "He had one of the spells that are occurring at least once or twice a day now."

"That breaks my heart," Carolina said, "I know he really wants to see Jake. Maybe if I talk to him, he'll snap out of it."

"I don't think that's a good idea," Adam said. "He's in bed, resting if not asleep."

"I'm sure you know best," Jake said. "Mom, Lizzie and I are staying the night at the Bent Pine. We'll try this again in the morning. For now I think we should just get out of here so we don't disturb him."

"Sorry to say it," Leif said, "but I think that would be for the best."

Mary made no move to leave. Instead she walked to the center of the spacious room. "You know, I remember dancing with Reuben in this very room. Furniture was different. Old fireplace looks the same, though.

"He had a Dean Martin song spinning on his

old Victrola." Mary started singing. "When the moon hits your eye… Sorry," she said. "I just got carried away."

Jake heard shuffling footsteps in the hallway. A minute later R.J. appeared at the door.

"Gwen, quit that squawking. Turn off that music and come to bed."

Carolina rushed over to take R.J.'s arm so as to help steady him.

"I'm sorry," Cannon apologized. "Dad frequently asks for someone named Gwen when he sinks into a confused state."

"He's not that confused," she said. "Reuben always called me Gwen. He didn't think Mary was a fancy enough name for me."

"Are you coming to bed?" R.J. insisted.

Tears moistened Mary's eyes. "No, you old fool. I'm not coming to bed. We're going to dance."

She walked over and put her arms around him. They swayed for a few seconds in each other's arms. "Now we're going to bed," she said. They walked away together, arm in arm.

"Well, I'll be damned," Adam said. "All this time we've been trying to figure out who the mystery woman Gwen was. Now it turns out she was his first wife."

Tears burned at the back of Carolina's eyes. R.J. and Mary, lovers from the past. R.J. called for Gwen when he faded to a place where he lost all sense of time and reality. Mary had called for R.J. when she was in a coma at the point of death.

Their marriage hadn't made it, but they must have loved each other very much at some point in the past.

Mary joined them a few minutes later. "Rueben's back in bed. I think we should go now. We'll come back in the morning. If he feels better I may even make him finish our dance."

CAROLINA AND MARY stood on the front porch at Dry Gulch waving goodbye to Adam, Jake, Lizzie and R.J. Carolina was thrilled with how the morning had gone so far. She should have known Jake and R.J. would have something to talk about. They were both ranchers.

R.J. couldn't wait to give Jake a tour of the Dry Gulch Ranch. That was where they were off to now, with Adam in the driver's seat.

Mary slapped her cheek lightly. "Wouldn't you know I walked right off and left that basket of peaches I brought for Reuben on your kitchen table back at the Bent Pine? I picked them myself just yesterday from my own trees."

"I can go back and get them," Carolina said.

"That's not necessary. He probably gets enough peaches from around here."

"Not ones that you've picked yourself."

And he would like that. It was easy to see he was excited about seeing her again.

"Are you okay here by yourself?" Carolina asked. "If not, you can ride back to my house with me."

"I'm just fine. Funny the little things I'm remembering just sitting here. The night I went into labor with Jake and we couldn't get our old car to start."

"What did you do?"

"Jake rode his horse over to a neighbor's in the middle of a thunderstorm and borrowed their car."

"Did you make it to the hospital in time?"

"About three days too early. It was false labor. Reuben didn't think it was nearly as funny as I did."

"I bet not. I'll drive over and pick up the peaches and be back long before the guys."

"Take your time, dear. I'll be just fine."

Carolina was already in the car and almost to the highway when she remembered that Jake had told her not to leave the ranch alone. He was still worried about Thad, but that was only because he was overprotective.

Even Sheriff Garcia had dropped by the ranch earlier this morning to tell them that Border Patrol had issued a statement saying they had credible evidence that Thad had escaped into Mexico.

The gate at the Dry Gulch was not automatic. She got out, pushed it open and then got back in the truck to drive through it. Then she had to get out and close it again.

She tuned the radio to one of her favorite stations that played a mixture of standards and light jazz. She liked driving her car again. Liked being home again, too.

If she and Jake were to marry, there would be a million changes she'd have to make in her life. She wouldn't see her grandchildren nearly as often. Most of her close friends lived nearby. Her doctors were all in Dallas. Her hairdresser was in Oak Grove. All the people she relied on for repairs or catering or altering clothes were in this area.

She glanced behind her as she neared the turnoff for the back road to the Bent Pine. A car was coming up on her fast. Too fast and it wasn't slowing down. She took to the shoulder to avoid being hit.

The car slammed into her. Her car skidded down the shoulder a good quarter of a mile before she could get it under control. When she looked in her rearview mirror, she could see the car was hanging back, as if the driver was waiting for the opportunity to hit her again.

This could not be a coincidence. Not on this road, where they had never had trouble like this before. Not so soon after Thad had run Lizzie off the road.

There was only one logical explanation. Thad Caffey wasn't in Mexico. He was in the car behind her and determined to run her off the road, the same way he had done to Lizzie.

Not very creative, but he'd probably figured that his best chance to get her alone was on this lonesome back road, either leaving or returning home. She had ignored Jake's warnings and played right into Thad Caffey's evil, murderous hands.

She floored the accelerator and steered hard around the curve. Just a few more miles, but she was approaching an even sharper curve.

She held on to the wheel with both hands. She was almost through the curve when she heard a gunshot. A second shot hit the back window of her car, shattering the glass into a million tiny fragments.

A new spray of bullets splattered the back of the car.

He was going to kill her, mere miles from the Bent Pine. She hit the curve going as fast as she could. The car practically went into orbit. It flew across the shoulder on the opposite side of the road and then started to roll. When it stopped, she and her car were upside down.

Vertigo struck with a vengeance. Her vision grew fuzzy and then went black.

By the time she revived and could focus again, she was on the ground, her hands bound at the wrists. Thad Caffey was standing over her, an ice pick clutched in his right hand.

Chapter Twenty-Three

Jake held on to R.J.'s arm to steady him as they walked to the truck from the horse barn. Lizzie was still bonding with every horse in sight.

"You've got some mighty fine horses," Jake said.

"That's my only claim to fame around these parts."

"Maybe not your *only* one," Jake said.

"Well, except for my bad reputation."

Jake's phone rang. It was Brad Pacer.

"I'm afraid I have to take this call," he said.

"Don't worry about me. I can still walk."

Albeit not very steadily. Fortunately, Adam came to the rescue.

"Morning, Brad," Jake said as Adam and R.J. walked away. "How are things in Brownsville?"

"I'm no longer in Brownsville. As of about two minutes ago, I'm on my way to Oak Grove."

"Why?"

"Thad Caffey was recently spotted in a service station about ten miles south of there."

The pressure swelled, pushing against Jake's chest.

"I'm not sure how credible this particular sighting is," Pacer admitted, "but I stopped everything to alert you."

"Thanks. I'll call you back later, but right now I need to make sure Carolina is not in danger."

He punched in Carolina's mobile phone number. There was no answer. His throat tightened. He called his mother. Thankfully she answered on the first ring.

"I'm trying to get in touch with Carolina. She's not answering her phone. Is she with you?"

"No, she drove back to the Bent Pine to pick up some peaches I forgot to bring with us this morning."

"How long has she been gone?"

"About ten minutes. You sound upset. Is anything wrong?"

"I don't know. Stay put, Mom. Don't leave that house."

He called the Bent Pine. Carolina's aunt Pearl answered. "Is Carolina there?" he asked.

"No, she left with you over an hour ago."

"You're sure she's not there."

"I'm sure I haven't seen her."

"Can you look in the kitchen and see if there's a basket of peaches on the counter?"

"They're still here."

"Thanks, Pearl."

Jake ran to Adam's truck. "I need to borrow your truck. It's urgent."

"Take it. I can get one of the wranglers to pick us up and drive us back to the house." Adam handed him the key. "Is there anything I can do?"

"Call Sheriff Garcia. Tell him Thad Caffey is in Oak Grove and Carolina is on her way from the Dry Gulch Ranch back to the Bent Pine. Send backup to the area ASAP."

"Did you say Thad Caffey has Carolina?" R.J. asked in a quivering voice.

"Hopefully not. But I'm taking no chances. I'm out of here now."

"Damn straight, you gotta go. Don't you dare let anything happen to Carolina. You kill that Thad Caffey. Do you hear me?"

"I hear you loud and clear."

Jake jumped into the truck and took off, following the dirt road all the way to the gate.

If anything happened to Carolina… No, he couldn't indulge in horrifying possibilities. He would not lose Carolina.

STILL DAZED, CAROLINA was only vaguely aware of the sticks and rocks scraping her back through her clothes as Thad dragged her through the woods.

"What do you want from me?" Carolina asked. "Why are you doing this?"

"You know why, you rich bitch. You meddle in other people's lives because you've got no life of your own. You talked Mildred into pressing charges against me and then divorcing me. I spent four long years in prison because of you. But you won't meddle in my life or Mildred's any longer."

There would be no reasoning with him. She had to outsmart him or find a way to break free. If she could run, at least she'd have a chance.

Finally he stopped walking and dropped her head and shoulder to the hard earth so hard she felt her brains had been scrambled.

Still, she tried to roll away from him. He yanked her back toward him by her long hair. Before she could try to fight him off, he straddled her and began running the tip of an ice pick along her neck and then down to the swell of her breasts.

A prick here. A prick there, painful, bloody reminders of what the ice pick could do if he pushed with more force.

She could see the evil burning in his eyes and she knew for certain what no one had been able to prove. He had killed his mother and his sister. Nothing in his past could justify that.

And now he was going to kill her. She screamed, but there was no one around to hear her.

She should have listened to Jake. And she should have told him she loved him. She did love him, so very much. Now all those unfulfilled dreams were about to die at the hands of a madman.

She closed her eyes, and as the tip of the ice pick slid between her breasts and down her belly, her mind escaped to the thrill of Jake's kiss and the joy of waking up in his arms.

ADRENALINE AND FEAR pushed Jake into overdrive the second he saw Carolina's ditched car. He searched the vehicle to make sure she wasn't still inside it, injured or...

No. She was alive. She had to be alive.

Convinced she wasn't still trapped in the car, he headed to the woods, his pistol at his hip, ready. He found their trail in seconds. One person walking. One person or thing being dragged. Did Jake dare call out or would that only startle Caffey and spur him into doing something desperate?

Jake kept walking, listening for any sound that might lead him to Carolina. The sound was a bloodcurdling scream. He took off, running as fast as he could. If Caffey had hurt Carolina, he'd kill him.

He reached Carolina just in time to see Caffey's hand raised high above his head, a bloody ice pick clutched in his fist. He was in position to plunge that thing right through her heart.

Acting on instinct, Jake dived into Caffey like a plane coming in for a crash landing. They struggled for the ice pick until Jake was able to subdue him. Jake was on the verge of finishing Caffey off with the same deadly kitchen utensil he'd been about to use on Carolina.

"Don't," Carolina begged. "Please don't. He's the one lost to the devils in his mind. We're the sane ones."

Jake's hand trembled, but he forced himself to lower his arm. He tossed the ice pick into the wooded area, but kept Caffey pinned to the ground, sputtering curses.

Jake turned to Carolina. "Are you okay, baby?"

"I am now."

"You're bleeding."

"Just barely. He was still into the torture phase."

"You need an ambulance."

"I won't turn one down, but it's strictly precautionary."

A few seconds later, Sheriff Garcia arrived on the scene. Tague was a few steps behind him.

"You're too late for the action," Jake said, "but I could use some handcuffs over here." Jake left Thad in the hands of Garcia. He sat down on the damp, pine-strewn earth beside Carolina and freed her wrists before pulling her into his arms. Jake buried his face in Carolina's hair. "Let's make a pact. Don't ever scare me like that again. My heart can only take so much."

"It's been a rough morning. As soon as I finish getting checked out at the hospital, I'll be ready to go home," she whispered.

"Where is home?"

"Anywhere you hang your Stetson on the hat rack and park your boots under my bed."

His heart hammered against his chest. "Do you mean that?"

"I've never meant anything more. I love you, Jake Dalton. I never thought I'd ever love again. Never imagined I could fall this hard so quickly. But when I thought I might die tonight, I knew that I had already given you my heart."

"I love you, Carolina Lambert. Now, who do I ask for your hand in marriage?"

"My three sons. I'll make sure they say yes."

Miracles. Sometimes you wait and wait for one that never comes. Other times one's right there when you need it. But on really rare occasions, they rain down on you like a spring shower.

This was one of those times.

* * * * *